Elizabeth Wambheim

More Than Enough

FOR YOU

More Than Enough

Prologue

"*Y*OU MAY EXCUSE YOURSELF AFTER MIDNIGHT, but not before."

"I know."

"You've made it this long, you can make it until then."

"I know."

"No one here is trying to antagonize you."

"Eckhart, I *know*."

"Good. Take a deep breath."

Fier, for once, followed instructions without protest and drew in breath enough to expand his narrow chest. As he exhaled slowly through his nose, the tension loosened from his shoulders, and Eckhart could see, briefly, Fier as he had been seven years ago, when the weightiest of his responsibilities had been sitting-room recitals on the grand piano.

The tumble of red-orange half-curls retained its waves, the flare of them more tameable in recent years, and the lines of his cheek and jaw had yet to settle into the sharp and fine-boned face he was destined to have in adulthood. He moved forward into the press of his guests with the same long-limbed grace he'd grown into so early and so easily. Mannerisms remained: the way he tilted his head to better hear the two violins of the quartet; the unconscious straightening of his spine as he addressed a guest, as if forgetful of the fact that he was already the taller of the two.

But more had changed than remained the same. Somewhere between fourteen and twenty-one, the prince's gait had lost the high steps of youth; his hands, once the cause of a thousand chastisements – "Don't touch, eyes only, that's fragile" – hung still and lifeless inside their black velvet gloves. And his eyes, without Eckhart ever seeing the change, had faded from the full green of spring to a sharp and steely jade.

He bowed, stiff and formal, to his first partner: a young lady with an ice-melting smile. *Please let this one go well,* Eckhart pleaded, praying to any deity with

2

the capacity to listen and attend. *Please. Just once.*

"Eckhart, sir." A hand on her shoulder drew her attention from the commencement of the dance. The attendant at her elbow, dressed in the requisite black and grey, spoke again: "We managed to salvage the letter from this morning."

"Is it legible?"

"This *is* Her Majesty's hand, sir; the script was largely impossible to begin with. But the ink did run less than we expected, and we were able to puzzle out most of the original text."

Eckhart closed her eyes, exhaled slowly. "Tell me she just wants to know how he's doing."

"She says the expenses involved in this ongoing endeavor have exceeded what is reasonable; this is the last promenade she will allow."

As much as she'd expected an ultimatum, the official pronouncement of it still turned Eckhart's blood cold. She returned her attention to Fier, who had been swept away from the dark-haired beauty and now stood just beyond the reach of a slender woman with auburn, clipped hair. This was their last chance.

"He refuses to hold court, you know." This was hardly the place or time to admit as much, but Sir Eckhart spoke at a volume low enough to discourage any eavesdroppers from attending. "He sits for it, but he won't address even the simpler problems anymore."

3

Beside her, the attendant shifted his balance from one foot to the other. "With all due respect, sir, your prince is a brat."

"He *will* be a good king." Eckhart knew the claim rang hollow, the words empty after too many fruitless repetitions, but the alternative was unthinkable. "He just needs to grow into it."

Though he laced his hands politely behind his back and kept his shoulders squared, the attendant still managed to shrug. His more nuanced disagreement, perhaps, would be more forthcoming in a less-public venue.

Eckhart lifted her gaze from Fier, who still hesitated to take his partner's proffered hand, and scanned the room at large. Since sunset, the scene had changed little, but even after several hours, the parade of young and beautiful courtiers remained as dazzling and beautiful as a garden in full bloom. Outside, the rain of early winter may have been lashing the windows all day, but here, safe indoors, was the flush of spring.

Dresses and tailcoats in vivid colors, forever the territory of the rich, caught the light: green and blue enough to rival the summer sea, red and orange swirling through like windblown sparks, and yellow sun-bright in the gaps between. The charcoal grey of the servants' formal uniforms were scattered around the border of the room, half of them invisible in the shadows of the corners.

Above everything hung the chandelier, heavy with crystal and candles, the whole of it glowing with spokes of gilded fire, a great bloom of light radiating a halo of gold.

A great expense. She could almost hear the words in Her Majesty's voice. That smooth, presumptuous tone ruffled the knight still, even after three years of its absence; such was a voice not accustomed to any listener's disregard. No one argued with the queen.

A great expense, when the price was a handful of copper pennies compared to the wealth lavished upon Fier's six older siblings. *A great expense* – when Her Majesty already pretended this backcountry manor was in any way equal to the cost of her other children's palace holdings.

This was their last chance. Eckhart set her jaw and closed her eyes for the space of a steadying breath. Of all she'd overcome on Fier's behalf, they could not be blockaded here. Tonight would fall as it may; they could reassemble the pieces in the morning.

"Don't *touch* me!"

The all-too-familiar words tore through the rustle of voice and fabric, and Eckhart's attention snapped back to the dancefloor even as she stepped forward to intervene.

"I said *don't!*" Louder this time. Guests fell silent, turned to look. The string quartet stuttered to a halt. Eckhart ducked and twisted between the slowing dancers.

"I barely even--"

"Just *stop!*" Fier's voice lifted again in open, strident distress. "Why is it so hard to *listen?*"

There. As if at the center of a small explosion, Fier and his partner, a freckled redhead blushing as dark as her hair, stood in the middle of a ring of their increasingly alarmed peers. Fier stood with a shoulder hiked, one hand against the nape of his neck and the other arm hooked around his ribs as if he'd been stabbed. The young lady had stepped back and kept her hands tucked against her chest, evidently more perplexed than upset.

Eckhart wedged herself between the two and, as Fier recoiled as if struck, dropped a hand to the pommel of the sword at her hip. "What happened?"

"Nothing." Fier shot a glance at his partner. "It was nothing."

Eckhart caught the prince's wrist, pried his arm away from his midsection. No blood – no injury. "Look at me."

But the prince kept his gaze averted. He tried, in vain, to wrench his arm from Eckhart's grasp. "Nothing happened. Let me go."

"He said it was nothing," the prince's partner put in. Her face was still flushed, and her hands were still curled inward as if they were weapons to be held in check. "It was a– a misunderstanding."

Nothing. Always nothing. Fier tried again to pull his arm free, and Eckhart let him go. "You need to--" Her voice was too clipped; she tried again: "Your Grace, please – none of this tonight. We need to--"

Fier jerked away – breaking free from the conversation as forcefully as he'd broken his keeper's grasp – and, without preamble, stalked through the parting crowd. Eckhart would have been content, in some capacity, to allow Fier to disappear into his room, even if the diplomatic consequences of the prince's dramatic departure caused far more ill than good. But Fier made no move for the staircase that led to the upper floors: he pushed his way toward the front door instead.

The young lady whispered an apology, but Sir Eckhart ducked after her ward with a lack of diplomacy that stuck like a needle in her throat. She would not argue, not in front of so many strangers, but neither would she allow the prince to disappear into the middle of a rainstorm.

She reached the foyer just as Fier's hand touched the latch, and as the prince began to draw open the door, Eckhart slammed a hand against it, forcing it closed again with a crack that rattled the sconces.

Despite the sound, despite the intervention, the prince did not flinch, did not release the handle of the door, did not seem at all to register Eckhart's presence.

"Fier. Please. Tell me what's wrong."

"I need to go outside."

"Not in the rain. Not like this."

"I have to go." His voice hitched higher; his breathing, already unsteady, turned fast and shallow. "Just let me go."

"Not in the rain. Your room is--"

"*No.* Not my room. I need to go."

"Why--" Eckhart broke off the question, surprise fluttering to life in her chest: Fier's hands were shaking, a condition mitigated only in part by his iron-tight grip on the door. "Fier, no one came here tonight to hurt you. No one means you any harm."

"I need to go."

Eckhart, silent, watched the prince's shaking carry from his hands to suffuse the rest of his body. This was not, as the rumors would insist, a tantrum. This – whatever it was – was something far, far worse.

But the storm was still raging outside; even if Fier would not go to his own room, he could not go out of doors.

Eckhart exhaled a deep, settling breath. "Stay, Fier. You are safe here. We can find somewhere else for you to sleep." She lifted her hand from the door. Fier, though he did not let go of the handle, made no move to flee. Hoping the worst had passed, Eckhart put a hand on Fier's wrist to guide him away from the threshold and the storm beyond.

The prince lashed out – faster than a snake – and Eckhart stumbled back in surprise, her cheek stinging.

For a heartbeat of stunned disbelief, she could do nothing but stare while Fier stared back at her, wild-eyed and open-mouthed. Realization caught his breath in the same moment it caught in her chest: He had struck her.

Tap tap tap.

Another moment passed in heavy silence before Eckhart recognized the sound for what it was: someone outside, requesting entry. Though she could feel a bruise already forming on her cheek, she turned to face the door and pulled her stance back into that of a responsible attendant. The movement must have startled Fier out of his shock, as he replaced his hands on the handle and slowly, slowly drew open the door.

A cold wind swept through the foyer. Hooded against the railings of the storm, framed by the pool of candlelight that flooded onto the doorstep, stood a hunched figure in a rain-soaked grey cloak. From what could be seen of the figure's face, wrinkled and shadowed though it was, the stranger was a woman far, far older than most of their usual visitors.

Before Eckhart could ask her business, she raised a clawed hand to proffer a small, once-perforated stone balanced on her palm.

"A token, Your Grace." Her voice was a clash of discordant sounds grating against Sir Eckhart's ears, but the words were clear enough. "In exchange for something warm to eat."

In the doorway, Fier's mouth tilted into a frown of obvious distrust. His breath fogged in the frigid air. He remained still and silent, his hair and clothes whipped by the tumult of the storm. Eckhart, suppressing an instinct to help, bit her tongue to keep from swaying the prince's course.

"I think," Fier began at last, voice low and ice-cold, "that I don't want anything you have to offer."

But as Fier began to close the door, the old woman, with speed not her due, lurched forward and closed her claw-like hand over the prince's gloved one. At once, Fier's shoulder hitched again, his whole body rigid. With instinctive immediacy, Eckhart stepped into his path, and even as the prince twisted free and raised his hand to strike the stranger, Eckhart seized his wrist—

The woman's hand closed over the stone—

A blinding flash of lighting tore through the clouds, on its heels a crack of thunder that slammed into Eckhart's ears like a physical blow, and as she blinked back bruised afterimages, the woman's form billowed outward in a miasma of dark smoke.

Fier cried out in pain or alarm or both, his arm vanishing from Eckhart's grasp —

The candles in the sconces sputtered out —

And Eckhart could hear nothing but the rain.

Petra

ONCE UPON A TIME, they said, as if they had not yet been born when the happenings transpired.

Once upon a time, they said, as if to turn the already-inexplicable truth into something even more mysterious.

Once upon a time, they said, *there lived the Queen and the King and their seven children.*

The first pair, girl and boy, were brave and tall in valor. The middle pair, girl and boy, were diplomatic and tall in eloquence. The last pair, girl and boy, were just and tall in wisdom. The Queen and the King knew that, when it came time to abdicate, any of their six eldest children would suit the throne.

But the seventh child, though the youngest and most beautiful, was known throughout the sovereignty as a monster. He spoke in rudeness. He disdained company. He refused to heed his tutors. The older he grew, the more monstrous he became, until to keep his company was to threaten a thunderstorm.

The Queen and the King, in their wisdom, saw fit to give each of their children the chance to prove themselves worthy of the throne. Each of the seven was given the governance of a town, and at the end of three years, whichever had governed with the gentlest hand, and the most perceptive eye, and the fairest rule would be the chosen heir.

"And *we* got the seventh prince."

"But he was bad!"

"And whenever someone went to him for help, he gave them terrible advice."

"Like what?"

"Well, when two farmers were arguing about who owned a foal, the prince told them to cut it into two pieces, right down the middle."

Giggles cut through the peaceful spring afternoon, accompanied by the splash of bare feet in the fountain basin. Petra set down his handful of moss and listened with one ear to make sure neither child had fallen in. But as the splashing subsided and the conversation rekindled, he relaxed and resumed his work.

"What else did he do?"

"One of the farmers wanted to know what to do about the weeds destroying her crops, and the prince told her to ask for help from someone else."

And so it went, and so Petra pretended not to listen. He folded thick, viridian moss into the basket in his lap, careful of the sharp edges of the basket's wire frame. Gloves would, of course, have protected his hands, but they made him clumsy, too, and so Petra worked bare-handed, the moss soft as fleece against his fingertips.

First the moss, then the soil: pockets of earth added together with the flowering seedlings carefully pressed through the moss and artistic tangle of wire. Most were marigolds, their first golden petals tinted scarlet, but Petra liked the alyssum best: handfuls of tiny white and pale blue flowers that smelled like honey.

"But one night, during one of his parties, a poor beggar knocked on his door and asked to be let in. The prince called her old and ugly and turned her away – but she was a *witch*. So she cursed him forever and ever and ever to be as *beastly* on the outside as he is on the inside."

Ageratum, too, would have been a natural choice, given how profuse they were with their downy lilac flowers, but most of the town asked for red and gold and white – the royal colors. The youngest prince may have failed them, but still they kept their trust in the rest of the family.

"And the next thing anyone knew, all the guests and all the household were outside. Anyone who tried to go back into the manor to get out of the rain couldn't take more than three steps over the threshold.

"But when Sir Eckhart couldn't find the prince anywhere, she ran back in – all the way in – and she was gone for hours. The guests had all been helped home before she came back out, shaky as a new foal, and she wouldn't say anything about what she'd seen. No one has been able to get in since, but sometimes you can see the shadow of the beast at sunset as he walks past the windows."

"*He* goes inside, though." The younger child's voice had dropped to a conspiratorial whisper, but Petra heard all the same, kept his head bent low over the last of his planting. "*He*'s never scared."

"Yes, well, he doesn't really count."

"Why not?"

"He's a witch." As if, at last, concerned about being overheard, the older sibling had softened her voice, but not nearly enough. "Witches aren't scared of anything."

Blossoms and leaves filled the basket to the point of overflowing, and the weight of them staggered Petra as he struggled to his feet. A borrowed chair creaked under his weight as he hefted the basket up and up and onto the hook in the alcove adjacent to the front door. Its mirror, the product of the morning's work, hung in the opposite alcove; bees already swirled around the new flowers, curious in their clumsy, rambling way.

Petra had long since given up trying to scratch the dirt out from beneath his fingernails, but he dusted his hands on his apron and brushed the worst of the scattered soil from his trousers. He also made a great deal of extra noise in stomping the dirt from his boots, but even so, as he rounded the corner of the house to step into the high-walled garden behind, the sisters looked up, startled, from where they sat on the lip of the fountain. The eldest curled her bare toes in the water, and Petra thought she looked paler than usual beneath her riot of freckles.

"Asa?"

She flinched, and a blush flooded her face from ear to ear.

"Would you tell your mother when she comes home that I've finished planting her flowers?"

"Y-yes, sir."

The younger of the two, darker than her sister, was small enough yet that she stared at Petra without a shred of self-conscious embarrassment, but Petra kept his chin tilted now without prompting, and whatever the girl could see of his face, it was not what she was looking for.

"Thank you, Asa. I'll be going now."

"Good-bye, sir. Thank you, sir."

He turned and retrieved his now-empty basket of supplies, walking fast enough to outdistance the new rustle of whispers behind him. But the words were repeated so often in so many voices that Petra did not need to hear them again in order to feel their sting.

Is that why he can go in the manor? Because he's beastly, too?

Maybe the prince is afraid of him.

Was he born that way? Or is he also cursed?

"Petra. There you are."

Petra stumbled to a stop, the basket bumping against his knees. He'd made it only a matter of steps from the low sandstone wall surrounding the siblings' home, and even though he knew he was still the topic of conversation in the garden behind, Petra set his jaw and turned to face the approaching Sir Eckhart with a polite and expectant frown.

"Marta told me you might still be here." Eckhart slowed to a stop on the brick lane, her hands folded behind her back and her spine a straight, straight line. "You have a visitor."

Ah. Petra hitched his basket up over his arm again. "Which kind?"

"One of the party-goers."

In their way, returning guests were far easier to deal with than the dismissed servants, especially with Eckhart's help. Petra nodded, and Eckhart, having waited for such a signal, turned on her heel and strode back the way she'd come. With the ease of much practice, Petra fell in behind.

The prince dead had aged Eckhart more rapidly than the prince alive ever had. The last three years had threaded her once-glossy black hair with grey, and the shadows under her eyes seemed darker with each passing season. But her sleek and military bearing persisted unchanged, and Petra almost had to jog to keep up with her long-legged steps.

And so the seventh prince was lost, to death or worse. His manor stands empty at the heart of his tiny province, a grand and silent warning, great shadows passing behind the dark windows.

Some would add, with needless cruelty, that the prince went unmourned, but those who claimed so had never, Petra knew, met Sir Eckhart.

No matter how often he entered the knight's cottage, the only change Petra could ever find was the fluctuating pile of letters on the heavy oak desk. Golden flowers on the windowsills bloomed year-round (with, of course, Petra's influence); the dark, almost black, wood of the walls and floor gleamed in the absence of dust or wear; a tattered royal banner hung behind the desk, the only formal decoration in a home otherwise austere.

As Petra stepped inside, the visitor, initially perched in one of the parlor's two overstuffed chairs, rose at once and dropped into an elegant sweep of a curtsy. Sunlight filtering in through the uncurtained window turned her braided hair and traveling cloak a soft, soft yellow.

"Master Gardener," she began, even before Petra could set down his basket, "I was told you —"

He tilted his head, but not fast enough, and as the young woman straightened from her curtsy, as she caught sight of his face, Petra could see untempered surprise cloud her features. Surprise darkened to veiled discomfort, and she did not, of course, look at him again. Not even now that he'd turned so she could not see in full the right side of his face.

"Petra, this is the Lady Celandine." Eckhart gestured with one gloved hand for the young woman to sit, but she remained upright, her hands clasped nervously. "My lady, if you would explain your situation as you explained it to me."

The young woman nodded but, not yet recovered, did not respond. Clearly she regretted her show of surprise, but no exhibition of court manners could undo her lapse in composure. Petra watched her struggle for politeness and tried not to think of the moss caught beneath his fingernails or the earth caked into the soles of his boots.

Her hands stilled, finally, and then she began to speak in a low, steady voice, as if she'd rehearsed the words: "There were so many of us, I don't think you would remember, but I was a guest at Prince Fier's final party those three years ago. I did not dance with him, although I had hoped to.

"Late in the evening, after the dancing began, I slipped upstairs to his bedroom and left my ring on the nightstand as a token. I took nothing," she added quickly, in response to a chastisement that had not come. "I only wanted a way to stand out from the other young women in attendance. I thought that if I left the prince something of mine, he would think of me more often than any of the others.

"I returned to the ballroom with none the wiser. Almost as soon as I stepped off the last stair, the... outburst happened." She glanced, briefly, at Eckhart, who nodded to encourage her to continue. "I gave my ring next to no thought, either then or in the years following. In truth, I would not pursue its recovery at all, except that I want very much now to give it away in earnest.

"It's a simple ring, just a thin golden band with etched petals. Even with the... the rumors, I don't know why it wouldn't still be on the nightstand. I know you're the only one who can go inside the house. Please, *please* bring it back."

Petra, then, glanced at Eckhart, who nodded again in silent encouragement, her expression carefully blank.

"I'll look for it. If it can be found, you will have it by this time tomorrow."

The young woman closed her eyes and let out a deep, shaking breath. "Thank you." She ducked into a hasty bow, her braid coiling over her shoulder. "Thank you, sir – from the bottom of my heart."

Petra wrapped his arms around the empty gardening basket and flattened it against his chest. "Do not thank me yet."

Fier

STARS. Fier had never seen so many stars. They flick-ered like pinpricks of candlelight, and he could almost see them shifting as one slow, giant pattern in the deep, velvet expanse overhead. Vertigo hooked into his chest; he closed his eyes. Anything to keep from falling into that dizzy, tumbling abyss.

He had been here before. He had always never seen so many stars.

Someone laughed – softly, secretly – and with that cue came music blooming out of the silence, the sound smooth and bright and familiar. Violins. The hook in his chest eased, and someone's hand found his, and a weightless, restless compass needle swung at last to north, and he fell into the sweeping steps of the dance as if, finally, this was home.

He had been here before. Always, he heard the laughter, the waltz.

He couldn't see her face, not even her eyes,

through the slits in her leonine mask. Its mane fanned and curled in waves of burnished copper; its mouth twisted up at the corners in a feral smile.

She'd been a snake, a wolf, a dove. Her mask changed – perhaps even her face changed – but she did not.

"I've been here before." His voice sounded muted, far away.

Another laugh. She tapped her fingers against his shoulder. "I should hope so, Your Grace. You live here."

He didn't. Absolutely he didn't. They spun across a wide, flat lawn nothing like the gardens he knew. No flowers. No trees. No fountains. Only a wall, waist-high, ringing the great gathering space with grey stone. Arbors of wood and latticework stood without greenery; they trailed strands of paper lanterns instead of ivy. Other guests, likewise masked, danced through light and shadow, but even in the light, their clothes looked vague and ill-defined. The details drew themselves in only as he sought them out.

He didn't live here.

And yet, sometimes behind them, sometimes beside, the black silhouette of the manor loomed. The windows were dark and dirty, and Fier knew better than to believe there was anything safe or familiar about that house.

The hand on his shoulder, so light he had forgotten it was there, tugged at the fabric of his collar. "Eyes on me, prince."

He tried to stand still, to let go of her, but the hand in his tightened and drew him stumbling into another step. The hand on his shoulder crept toward his neck, and Fier froze mid-spin, skin prickling.

"Stop." His voice was still wrong, still distant.

Another laugh. "Stop what?"

"I don't--" She ghosted her hand up the back of his neck, and Fier shuddered, ducked his head away from her invasive touch. "*Don't*-- do that. Don't."

"You needn't be coy, Your Grace."

He was beginning, as always, to feel tense and sick, as if at any moment he might actually be ill. He wouldn't overreact – not this time, not again.

But she found again the edge of his collar, and Fier's stomach lurched up into his throat, and in a volcanic rush of alarm, he wrenched himself free and shoved her away from him with a force he didn't intend. She stumbled backward into another guest. The movement dislodged her mask and it fell and behind it, she had no face at all.

Then she was the witch – the stooped old woman with lightning in her eyes and her proffered stone exploding into black smoke—

He woke, gazing this time into a void without stars, nothing but an ache in his chest to tell him he wasn't dead.

How long had he been here? Where was Sir Eckhart? Where was the witch?

Something slithered past, darkness on darkness, and Fier felt a too-familiar churning of fear and sickness twist through his heart. He curled in on himself, hoped he was likewise invisible in the gloom, and the shadow passed. He could still feel his heart beating rabbit-fast, but the breathless, mindless panic eased. It was gone. He was safe, until it wandered back.

Slowly, the lines etched in gradually as his vision adjusted, Fier could make out the edges of a bed and a great oak wardrobe rising up from the floor like a behemoth, its doors ajar. A grey-black rectangle at the foot of the bed must have been a trunk – his trunk. This was his bedroom.

This might well have been another dream. The hazy edges of the garden masquerade were gone, as was the persistent sense of déjà vu, but nothing in this place felt quite real, either. *He* didn't feel real. The masked woman's hands had been cold and heavy, but here, he could feel nothing at all: he knew where his hands ought to be, but they had no shape or weight; he knew where his legs ought to be, but those, too, seemed absent. He couldn't feel anything at all except for the tight, tight knot of his heart.

Maybe he *was* dead.

Something in his mind slipped out of place, tilting him out of his bedroom, and he fell down, down, down, out of the room and away.

Stars. He had never seen so many stars.

Petra

EVEN IN THE SOFT, ROSY LIGHT OF MORNING, the manor looked cold and forlorn. Calling it haunted had never struck Petra as the proper term. *Lonely* seemed more accurate. It stood tall and square and silent in the heart of its now-wild gardens, ready to be a home again, should someone come back to it. Ivy crowded the brickwork and birds built their ramshackle nests in the eaves, but Petra knew as well as anyone that plants could not serve as a replacement for human company.

Standing before the half-open front door, Petra touched the leather cord at his neck and exhaled. Find the ring and leave. Think of nothing else.

With one step, he crossed the threshold and drew in a deep breath. The air was thicker, heavier, and for that first gasp, Petra grew dizzy for lack of air. The next breath was easier as his body adjusted, and by the third, he could breathe as easily as if he still stood outside.

An enchantment, Eckhart had called it. Petra ran his hand absently across the surface of the foyer table and gave his fingers a cursory glance. No dust. Not even after three years. *Something in that place slowed time – or stopped it altogether.*

Certainly, nothing had changed here since the night of the curse, except for the blanket Petra had draped over the ornate mirror hanging opposite the front door. The trail of old dirt on the otherwise polished floor was evidence of Petra's prior wanderings, and in the darkest rooms, he'd thrown back the curtains for light enough to see by. Beyond that, books remained arrayed neatly on their shelves and the rooms' furniture, with upholsteries rich in reds and golds, lay smooth and unruffled by errant fingers.

With only the scuff of his boots on the wooden floor for company, the echoes painfully loud in the wide and empty rooms, Petra wound his way through the ballroom (noticeably cold in the absence of other people) and up the arching staircase to the floor above, and then up once more to the third and final landing. In all his wanderings through the manor, from attic to cellar, Petra had never gone into the prince's bedchamber, though he knew it from the intricacy of the carvings on the not-quite-closed door: spiraled vines and many-petaled flowers and long, looping stems – a garden nearly as untamed as those beyond the front door. Tulips, the town's flower of choice, took up most of the door, but, in Petra's opinion, they lost much of their charm when seen without color.

There is something in there, Petra. Eckhart's warning and dark eyes flickered to the forefront of his mind. *I don't know how you escape its notice, but do not forget that you trespass in its home.*

Three years and he had never seen it. Three years, and Petra had not once set foot in the prince's room. As much as he knew the creature wandered, spied as it had been from multiple windows, the correlation came with a dread he could not shake. Sir Eckhart had survived the ordeal of meeting it face-to-face, but Eckhart could survive anything. Petra was just a gardener.

He touched the edge of the door with two fingers, held his breath, and pushed. The door swung open on soundless hinges.

The high ceiling and deep pockets of darkness resembled too much a cave, and Petra shrank back from the threshold. But, his eyes adjusted already to semi-darkness, he took in the grey silhouettes of bed and wardrobe and bedside table. Slivers of sunlight crept in between the edges of the windows' heavy drapes, but this room was as tired and empty as the rest of the house. Nothing moved.

The beast, then, was wandering still.

Three years of routine nudged Petra into the room and into action. He sidestepped the floor's ornate rugs to reach the curtains, and with the best grip he could manage on the thick velvet, dragged them out of the way.

Daylight lanced into the room, bright enough to sting. But sunshine helped, as it always did, and Petra turned back to the room with a much-weakened sense of dread. The nightstand at his hip, awash in new light, carried nothing except a cluster of old, circular stains from unattended, now-absent drinking glasses.

He looped around the bed to check the other table and found the ring there, as promised. There was nothing else on the nightstand, only the ring, and Petra felt a flicker of sorrow for the prince, bully though he might have been: the only suggestion that this room had once been lived in came from a trinket not even his, and even that was not to be the case for much longer.

Petra picked up the ring and rolled it between his fingers. The engraved petals flashed in the sunlight, as bright as if newly-made. He dropped the ring into his pocket and turned to leave.

And saw the flower.

It lay in the shadow cast by the bed, the stem

smooth and emerald green, the long, tapered petals caught in the sunset colors between copper and orange. It was not quite a chrysanthemum and not quite a lily, but as Petra crouched to examine it more closely, expecting to feel fabric or glass, he found the petals soft and yielding and almost warm.

He had found other living things in the manor before. Certainly there were no mice or spiders or even ants in the pantry, but a town in love with flowers had once, reluctantly, filled the prince's home with them, and into the curse they stayed: lilac stars and white flutes and crimson roses with sparks of yellow trailing across their petals. But Petra had taken these from the manor, one armful at a time, as florists and gardeners approached Eckhart to ask for them returned. Decorating the prince's home when he was alive, they said, was trial enough, but the best of their flowers would not be wasted on a haunted shell of a house.

Well, here, at least, was one flower the prince would be able to keep. Petra lifted it from the floor, cradled the curling petals in his palm. Once out of the shadows, it nearly glowed, more red-gold than coral, and while it had nearly no scent at all, it was nevertheless a breath of bright life in a house sadly without.

Petra set the flower on the newly-cleared bedside table where it would be fully in the path of advancing daylight. Though it was as surely paralyzed in time as everything else in the manor, a dreaming flower might still desire the sun.

"I'll bring a vase," he promised. "I'll come back tomorrow."

Checking once to make sure the ring was still in his pocket, Petra turned and followed the remnants of his own footsteps out of the room, through the house, and back into the breathing world beyond.

Petra

FOR A MOMENT, Sir Eckhart's home was a perfect painting of how Petra had seen it the day before. A flood of bright afternoon sunlight gilded the flowers on the windowsill. Dust motes drifted with a lazy ease on the still air. The Lady Celandine perched with courtly formality in one of the room's two chairs.

But this time, the young lady sat with her hands folded loose and calm in her lap. Sir Eckhart sat with an equal ease at her grand oak desk, her posture lacking the military sharpness of the day before.

They both glanced up as Petra stepped inside. Lady Celandine leapt at once to her feet and had nearly reached him before he could produce the ring from his pocket.

"You found it!" She closed his hand tightly in both of hers – warmer gratitude than Petra had expected. "Thank you – so, so dearly, thank you! I don't know how to repay you."

"You don't have to."

"Are you certain?" She looked at him now with none of the awkwardness of the previous afternoon, and that was more unsettling than the sincerity of her handshake. "Do you often refuse payment?"

As soon she released him, the ring in her palm, Petra folded his hands behind his back. "It was an easy errand. You owe me nothing."

"Then the beast really does leave you alone! I'd heard as much."

Behind her, Sir Eckhart's mouth compressed into a thin frown, and Petra swiftly changed the subject: "The flower you left him was beautiful."

"The flower?" The Lady Celandine's brow wrinkled. "What do you mean?"

"The orange one in the prince's room. That was a lovely gift."

The young lady's forehead creased further, but the corner of her mouth quirked upward in an uncertain smile. "I didn't leave any flower, and I didn't see one when I left the ring. Another guest must have gone in after I did."

"Oh." Petra tried, with limited success, to keep the disappointment from his voice. "I was going to ask the name of it."

That earned a laugh – light and good-natured. "It is a rare day when the best gardener in the town of flowers doesn't recognize one."

"If you have everything you need, my lady," Sir Eckhart cut in, rising from her desk, "I would be honored to escort you back to your carriage."

Petra could hear the tension edging the knight's voice, but the Lady Celandine, her eyes still bright with a smile, seemed blissfully unaware of any discomfort brewing beyond the bubble of her happiness. She waved away Eckhart's concern with her free hand, the other curled closed against her chest. "The carriage is only as far as the inn, my good sir. I can make my way there on my own."

Sir Eckhart bowed and the Lady Celandine responded with a deep curtsy. She favored Petra with a curtsy as well, and he managed a clumsy dip of his head and shoulders in reply. The lady's exit was threaded with far more happiness than many of her predecessors, and as she stepped out of the cottage in a shimmer of gold, Petra felt a minute flicker of envy for whoever she was returning home to.

"She needs the ring to propose," he guessed.

"Yes. From the sound of it, her beloved is an up-and-coming merchant – an enterprising young lady." Eckhart had come around the edge of her desk and stood with her arms crossed. Her gaze sharpened. "Tell me about this flower."

The knight's undivided attention always made Petra feel like an insect trapped in a jar, scrutinized with intensity and nowhere to hide. But he squared his shoulders and kept his eyes on the banner just past her head.

"It looked like a lily, but with too many petals," he began, and regretted already his inability to find appropriately poetic terms. "It was a very... soft orange, with a slender green stem and no thorns. I've never seen a flower like it, not in the manor or outside. I'd remember."

Eckhart's somber expression did not waver, but she relaxed in the careful and deliberate way that Petra knew disguised uneasiness. "Be careful of anything you don't recognize, Petra. It might be part of the curse, and an unattended flower is excellent bait for a gardener. I don't want you in more danger than you already are."

Petra knew better than to dismiss the warning, and he ducked his head with the semblance of obedience. But he knew magic when he saw it, and that flower burned with it.

Fier

"YOU LIVE HERE, Your Grace."

"I don't. I don't live here. I don't believe you."

"Why can't you trust me?"

"Because--" Her hand crept again past his collar; panic, never far out of reach, crept into his throat. He kept his eyes closed. "Because you're not real. I know you're not real."

But he could feel her fingertips frigid against the edge of his shoulder, cold enough to set him shivering. Nausea, too vivid to be a dream, tangled through his stomach and left him dizzy. Not this, not this, anything but this. Don't look, don't look, don't look.

"I promise, Your Grace, that I am very, very real."

"Leave me alone."

But of course, of course, she brushed her hand up the back of his neck, and Fier lashed out in blind panic, felt the metal of her mask bruise his knuckles, heard her cry of surprise. He screwed his eyes shut all the tighter, but still he could see her: first faceless, then as the witch, her cursed stone belching black smoke.

"Let me go." Vertigo pulled apart his thoughts. He was crouching in the grass – he was standing in the foyer – he was curled in on himself without a body but with a heart beating so hard it might burst. Blood rushed in his ears, louder than a thunderstorm. This was a nightmare and an endless one but he was alive and he could hear himself over the storm – "Let me go, let me go, let me go" – and as long as he was still talking, she hadn't killed him.

Slowly, slowly, slowly, his heartbeat settled. The dizziness passed. The storm eased. The panic tearing through his chest receded into his stomach and then dissipated entirely. It was over. For now it was over. He'd be pulled down again soon, he knew, but the respite was beautiful, whatever sliver of time it lasted.

But as he waited, tense, for the world to pull itself out of shape, nothing happened. Nothing happened. Wherever he was, he was going to stay.

Something tingled in his fingertips and in his chest, and Fier, after its absence for so long, did not recognize it at once for what it was: warmth. He was warm. Weak and tired, but warm.

After one beat of his heart, then two, then three, he opened his eyes, and nearly had to close them again against the sudden suffusion of light. The surprise faded, but the light did not, and as his eyes adjusted, the familiar shapes unfurled around him: bed, wardrobe, wide and unfettered windows.

He sat in the middle of his bedroom, as before, but sunlight poured in through uncurtained windows and set the whole room glowing. The wardrobe gleamed as if newly-polished, its metalwork shining like caught sparks. The scarlet of the rugs and the bedding and the tapestries seemed brighter now than they ever had in mornings before, and the air itself seemed as rich and gold and heavy as honey.

For all the fear laced in his blood, for all the recurring nausea that he had come to expect as a constant, Fier found his pulse steady. He was calm, dizzy with it. The light of the room wrapped around him like a new blanket and its gentle heat settled on his skin and sank into his heart. He was warm.

Footsteps in the hallway drew his attention to the door. Eckhart? One of the servants? Who would know he was here?

Wrapped in a haze of still-unfamiliar peace and ease, Fier made no move to stand as his visitor stepped into the room.

Compared to the tightly-controlled chaos of the capital, the manor was small and straightforward, and even without trying, Fier had memorized the names and faces of most of the regular servants. But this one, he did not know.

The young man wore the tan apron and breeches and faded green shirt of the royal gardeners, a familiar uniform, but as he stepped from the darkened hallway into the light, a shadow clung to his features: a smudge, a birthmark, maybe, across nearly the entire right half of his face, dark against the rich oak of his skin. And even if Fier had not remembered such a face, he would have remembered the eyes: brown and soft and kind, even if the rest of his expression held no trace of a smile.

"Oh." The gardener's frown deepened. "You fell down."

"I didn't," Fier protested, but as he levered himself to his feet, the gardener strode into the room, through Fier – his dark, close-cropped curls passing straight through the prince's nose – and knelt to pick something up from the rug beyond. A flower – he picked up a flower and twirled it thoughtfully between his fingers. He smiled, then, a tiny, private smile. He seemed as fond of the plant as only a gardener could be, and seemed, too, to be utterly oblivious to the prince, faintly puzzled, behind him.

"Stay here this time," the gardener whispered. Fier noticed, belatedly, that he carried a small glass jar of water in his other hand, and in this the gardener placed the flower before setting the improvised vase upon the bedside table in the full light of the sun.

On a whim, the prince stepped closer and moved to touch the jar, but his fingertips passed through the glass, just as easily as the gardener had passed through him. Was he a ghost? Had he died? He couldn't bring himself to panic; he felt too sleepy and too warm to manage more than a dull confusion. *Had* he died? His heartbeat he could feel like a drum in his chest, and if his heart still beat, surely he must still be alive?

"I'll check on you tomorrow. In case you've fallen."

The gardener touched the jar one final time, adjusting it just so, and turned to leave. Fier tensed, prepared for a confrontation, but the gardener strolled right through him a second time, as if the prince were made of nothing but air, and walked back through the room, out of the door and away, and Fier did not follow.

Petra

FOR ALL THE THINGS he had removed from the manor,
Petra had never brought and left anything inside, and
even if he had left only a scuffed and cloudy glass jar,
the back of his neck prickled with unease as he
crossed the grounds. Nothing had protested the intru-
sion, or stopped him from leaving, but still Petra
could feel eyes following him all the way through the
gardens. Only when he reached the gatekeeper's cottage and the manor fell out of sight did the feeling
subside, and Petra let out the breath he didn't know
he'd been holding.

Leave it be, Eckhart had said, but even with the
warning, and even with this new and unsettling feeling of being watched, Petra intended to do no such
thing. Plants held no malice; people did. Whatever
haunted the prince's manor was not housed in so
strange and lovely a flower.

Even so, the sense of invisible and persistent eyes
sent a belated shiver through him. If the same sense of

dread tailed him through the manor tomorrow, frequent visits would be more difficult than planned. But that was a knot to unravel tomorrow. For now, Petra nudged open the unlocked door of the cottage and skirted the thistles blooming in the cracks of the front step.

The tangled green smells of home wrapped around him at once, and Petra closed his eyes as he crossed the threshold, unease falling away as he drew in a breath so deep his lungs ached. He could hear the flutter and click of a songbird settling on the beams of the ceiling. The bees humming near the open window eclipsed the birdsong he had forgotten to listen for outside. A breeze blew from the window through the still-open door, brushing through Petra's hair and rustling the bundles of dried herbs hanging overhead.

With peace settling over him like a coat, Petra touched his collarbone, found the leather cord at his neck. He hooked a finger under it and drew it up from beneath his shirt until his fingers could close over its grey stone of a pendant.

A token for your kindness, little one. He ran his thumb along one rounded edge, the nail of the same hand only a little smaller than the stone itself. A hole worn through the center bound it to the cord. *Wear this and be safe.*

Be good, be brave, be kind. Petra looped the cord over his neck and hung the pendant on a nail above the door.

A bumblebee, soft and heavy, bumped into his shoulder, wobbled, and managed to loop her way around him and into the cottage. Petra closed the door and watched as his new guest made her way across the room to join her sisters at the sunflowers nodding beyond the window.

The sun may have been brightest in the cottage at dawn, but the room's flora grew rampant all the same. Tucked between the bundles of dried mint and thyme, small terracotta pots and bubbles of glass carried gardens in miniature: clean white chamomile flowers with sunburst hearts; clover, their petals softer cousins to the thistles; moss and thin slices of grass. Glass jars ranged along the windowsill, holding mint with its scalloped leaves or parsley's long stems or the thick and shining leaves of basil sprouting nearly too big now for its jar.

Petra stepped carefully around the half-barrel of tall, dark purple heather, adjusted a basket of sprouting sweet potatoes, and trailed his fingers through a henna plant's ruffled, cream-colored petals. The aloe, too, was growing too large for its pot: its huge, sharp-edged leaves curled protectively around new growth at the center.

He's a witch, you know, sir. He could still hear the equerry, loud and careless of how many people heard him. He could still see Sir Eckhart with her arms crossed and her mouth an increasingly deepening frown. *I've never seen where he lives, sir, but I've heard it's all plants, all poisonous things. He lives in a wild place.*

A sleeping mat on the floor served well enough as a place to sit, and Petra leaned against the heap of blankets Sir Eckhart had left one by one on his doorstep during the winter months.

For all of the assorted treasures he had removed from the manor, none had ever left him with so strong a sensation of being watched. If Eckhart was right and the flower was part of the curse, then something did *not* want him to interfere with it. A breath of air in an otherwise airless castle was not what had knocked the flower from the bedside table.

Sometimes, in the first warm days of spring, if Petra closed his eyes and held very still, he could feel the season change. He could feel, in the pit of his stomach and the soles of his feet, the unfolding of a world asleep: hundreds of seeds stretching tiny green sprouts up to a light they had no eyes to see, the earth warming under the kindness of a new sun, everything softening and relaxing and relearning how to breathe.

He felt that way now, even with spring in full flower. Something stirred. As inexorable as the tilt from one season to another, something reached for wakefulness and for a distant sun.

"DO NOT BE COY, Your Grace."

"Stop this."

Starlight.

"You live here, Your Grace."

Sunlight.

"Good morning. You fell again."

Curtains. The glass of his bedroom window. The sprawling gardens beyond. He tried to touch the window, and his hand passed through, but still he could feel the bloom of sunlight on his face and shoulders.

Stars. Fier had never seen so many stars.

Violins.

"I've been here before."

Sunlight.

The flower on the floor again, the jar rolled under the bed again, the gardener stepping into his room again.

"Eyes on me, Your Grace."

"I don't want this."

"Rain today, but you'll have sun tomorrow."

Fingers on his neck. Metal against his knuckles. Fingers on his wrist. His heart beating beating beating out of his body.

The slithering shadow, darkness on darkness in the void of his bedroom.

The gardener beyond the window, kneeling in the nearest flowerbeds, a thin twist of a seedling cradled in his hands. The corner of his mouth tipped upward in a mild and thoughtful smile. His eyes brown and soft and kind.

A lion. Always a lion now. Copper folds of mask and mane gleaming sharp and bright beneath the paper lanterns.

"You glow in the sunlight, you know."

Grey hair, grey skin, grey eyes. Smoke billowing up from clawed hands.

The gardener beyond the window. Caught in sunlight. Outlined in gold. He paused in his work, turned his face up to the unclouded sky, and, eyes closed, drew in a deep, deep, settling breath.

Petra

PETRA STEPPED OUTSIDE and nearly tripped over the covered basket on his doorstep. Eckhart's usual deliveries came in wicker boxes dusty with use, but this one wore its brass hinges and leather tab like a new uniform. He knelt and raised the lid.

Fabric caught the light – as rich and buttery a yellow as the Lady Celandine's cloak from three weeks ago. He tipped it from the basket and it cascaded across his hands to fall in heavy folds against his legs. It felt like a breeze against his fingertips: cool and impossibly smooth.

He should have known she would send a gift. Almost everyone did. The nobility left their impractical finery; the villagers left freshly-baked bread and secondhand boots.

Petra folded the cloth back into the basket and tucked the lot just inside the doorway. He would leave it for Eckhart to deal with, as she dealt with most of the things he had no use for.

Rain threatened again today, as it had for much of the week, but even with the gathering clouds and rising wind, and even as a few overeager droplets caught his nose and eyelashes, Petra supposed he could be in and out of the manor and holed up in the gatekeeper's cottage before the real storm started. As cold as the manor was even on sunlit days, the cloudy ones turned it frigid.

But he had promised himself to visit every day, and after three weeks, he would not shy from the promise now. Petra cut a path through the wet grass, pausing only at one of the less-overgrown of the ornamental ponds. Gold-and-silver fish darted beneath the lilies and nibbled at his fingertips as he knelt to fill an old tonic bottle, then feathered away like shooting stars as he stood to recork the bottle and replace it in the pocket of his apron. If today followed the same pattern as the twenty before, then the jar he'd left in the prince's room would be somewhere on the floor, as dry as if he'd left it untended for months.

The sensation of being watched had faded after those first few days, but still Petra's skin prickled as he stepped inside, and he half-expected his breath to fog with each exhale. Thunder crackled once, then settled. Petra touched the cord at his neck, felt the weight of the pendant against his chest. Nothing had happened to him before; nothing would happen to him now.

He threaded his way through the manor, habit more than will carrying him forward. The foyer, the sitting rooms, the ballroom (a cavern, echoing and empty), the staircase winding upward. Last of all, the top-floor corridor and the door to the prince's room. The door was always ajar now, even if Petra, upon departure, closed it tightly behind him. He pushed it the rest of the way open—and froze.

But even as his heart slammed up into his throat, Petra bit down against the sudden shock of panic. This wasn't the beast. This wasn't the beast.

He sat cross-legged on the floor, his back not quite against the frame of the bed, his face turned toward the window and the clouds beyond. Even with the day overcast, his skin bore the rich golden-brown glow of sunlit sand. His hands, gloved in what looked like black velvet, rested empty in his lap. The flower Petra had come to tend to lay unheeded at the young man's knee.

Petra had seen him once before. On the snow-laced winter morning six years ago when the manor's newly-collected staff had stood stamping their feet and shivering at the manor's gate in a frozen welcome party. Petra had stood at the back, sandwiched between the old master gardener and his fellow apprentice for warmth, and so he had caught only a glimpse of the new residents as they arrived: Sir Eckhart austere in dress and manner riding just ahead of her ward whose black-gloved hands twisted anxiously in the white silk of his horse's mane.

Then, as now, the crisp edges of the prince's waistcoat and cape, both the red and gold of royalty, stood at odds with the wild red-orange tumble of hair across his forehead and around his ears.

Then, as now, the clean and elegant lines of his face seemed especially sharp in the grey light. But, while his mouth and eyebrows had been drawn tight with checked emotion on that first day (and, according to the servants, every day since), the prince's expression now was distant and unseeing, his attention lost inward.

While Petra fought his startled pulse, the prince's unfocused gaze slid from the window to land on him, and, not sure what else to do, Petra held still. The prince blinked, and something like awareness flickered back into the pale green of his eyes. His mouth wavered into the beginning of a puzzled frown.

"You can see me?" His voice was hoarse; the words were slow.

"Yes, Your Grace."

Another blink – another ghosted frown. "Not that."

"Not what, Your Grace?"

"Fier or nothing."

Petra's mouth had gone dry, and all he could think of was that this was all somehow treasonous – the once-dead prince sitting on the floor while Petra stood, Petra trespassing in a now-occupied house, the suggestion that he address the prince with his unadorned first name – but he swallowed and answered anyway: "Yes, Fier."

If the prince heard, his expression did not change. He simply sat, hands still folded placidly in his lap, and stared at Petra as if he could not quite bring him into focus. Petra, accustomed to being stared at, returned the scrutiny and waited.

"Who are you?"

An expected question. "Petra."

"Where is everyone else?"

"They... left. Everyone left."

The prince shifted his gaze at last and focused instead on the empty air just to Petra's left. His frown deepened, presumably as he wrestled his thoughts into order and did not like what he found. "How long ago?"

"Three years. We thought you were dead."

"My parents – did they...?"

Sympathy hitched in Petra's chest. Eckhart's desk flashed to mind: the constant cycle of letters written and sent, written and sent, but none ever brought by the post in reply. "They never came," he answered, softening his voice as much as he could. "We sent word, but they never came."

The prince's expression wavered, then, between dreamlike vacancy and open pain, and more treasonous still than addressing the prince by his first name was seeing him so unguarded; as Fier raised his hands to hide his face, Petra looked at the wall-hangings instead.

The prince wasn't dead. Three years without a trace of him, and here he was, dressed for the dance that had ended with his disappearance as if no time had passed at all. What would his parents do? What would his siblings do? What, Petra wondered with a jolt, would *Eckhart* do? More than any of the rest of them, Eckhart should be told that the prince was alive.

Unless this wasn't the prince.

Petra had never traded so much as a word with Prince Fier before now, but the monstrous spoiled brat described by the servants and the townsfolk did not match up with this sad and lonely stranger slumped against the edge of the bed. Maybe the creature haunting the manor had learned to wear a face – had learned to lure in its prey with pretty eyes and a plea for kindness.

But *a token for your kindness, little one*, and as

there had been no real choice then, so there was no real choice now. Maybe this was a monster playing at being a human. Maybe it wasn't.

"Fier," he began, slow and careful, "Sir Eckhart will want to know you're alive."

"No!" Fier jerked his face up out of his hands, aghast. "Don't tell her."

Petra hesitated, not sure if he ought to be annoyed or alarmed by this response. "You don't know how much she's missed you. She thinks you're dead."

"I *am* dead."

Petra took his turn to frown, but Fier leaned back against the bed – *through* the bed – and Petra's stomach twisted. As solid and real as the prince had seemed at the start, so he remained, but the wooden frame of the bed passed straight through his shoulders. The joining was seamless, as if body and wood and cloth had always been combined, but the visual mismatch left Petra dizzy.

"You couldn't see me before," Fier added as he straightened. His eyes were brighter and less clouded. "I haven't been awake."

Petra glanced at the flower still tucked beneath the prince's knee, its petals too colored like the prince's loose curls to be chance. "You've been asleep?"

"I don't quite know." Again, the prince's expression

wavered between confusion and swallowed tears. "I keep having… a bad dream. Over and over."

Feeling as though he was walking across an increasingly thin and unsteady platform, Petra could not quite bring himself to ask for further clarification. He did not know what to do. The prince was alive – the prince was a ghost – the prince had been dreaming for three years – this might be a trap – the prince was holding his head in his hands again, his breathing shaky. Between the shifting rules of the manor's enchantment and the overwhelmed prince, Eckhart would know how to handle this. Eckhart, always so self-possessed, could sail through any tricky social entanglement with just the right words, the right response.

But Eckhart wasn't here.

Stiff from standing so long frozen, Petra stepped over the threshold on unsteady legs and took a seat at the prince's right side – not quite close enough to touch, even if they could.

"I won't tell Sir Eckhart if you don't want me to." Petra could hear Fier draw in a quick breath at that, but his face was still hidden by his gloved hands. "But you are not dead and this is not a dream."

"*You* might be a dream," was the muffled reply. The words, though accusatory, sounded more miserable than suspicious. "And you saw – I'm dead. I'm a ghost."

"You are not dead. You are under a curse."

"Same thing."

"Not so. Some part of you is still alive."

Fier tilted his head enough to shoot a bottle-green glare at Petra. "How would you know?"

"It's just... a feeling." Given Fier's continued frown, a *feeling* was not enough to serve as reassurance, but Petra could offer nothing else; he could only say again, this time in little more than a whisper, "You are not dead."

Whatever cloudiness had plagued the prince earlier was now all but gone. The object again of Fier's undivided attention, Petra found the prince's scrutiny similar to Sir Eckhart's: both were unblinking, as narrow in focus as that of a cat on the prowl. But where Eckhart seemed able to read and measure the shape of someone's soul at a glance, Fier seemed to know neither what he was looking for nor what to do with what he found.

"Who are you?"

"Petra."

With an impatient huff, Fier waved the answer away. "No, no, that's your name. What are you doing here?"

"Shall I go?"

"No. But you're the only one who hasn't left. Why?"

"There's no one else who can come inside."

"But you can?"

"Should I not?"

"You can if you like. I don't care. But why haven't you left?"

For the first time, Petra felt a flicker of the irritation that must have so plagued the household staff. He didn't want to give an answer, not to someone he barely knew, but Fier acted as if he was entitled to a reply, no matter how invasive the question.

"Shall I go?" he asked again, braced to stand.

He had tried to keep the hunted edge out of his voice, but Fier rocked back, as visibly stricken as if he'd been shoved. "Please – not yet." Panic kicked the prince's voice several notes higher. "I won't pry – I'm sorry. Don't go. Not yet."

Guilt lurched through Petra's stomach. Fier was newly-awake and, after three years of being trapped in a nightmare, finally not alone. He had awoken to find his body gone and everyone in his life absent – everyone except for one person whom he had never met. He had every right to want to know what had happened after he disappeared and why his only companion was a stranger.

"I'll stay," he promised. Pretending not to notice Fier's open sigh of relief, he continued: "After you... disappeared, everyone found themselves outside in the rain. Their gloves or coats or scarves were still inside. Guests tried to go in to fetch them, but they would take two or three steps in and then have to give up, they would be so terrified. Sir Eckhart managed to make it all the way in, but she--"

"She ran back in?"

"She went to look for you."

Fier bit his lower lip and turned his face to the window. Petra gave him space to reply, but when no response was forthcoming, he went on:

"Sir Eckhart was gone for hours, but she came back empty-handed. No one really tried after that. But Nadeen, the old master gardener, had left his hat in the kitchen. We didn't really think we could get it back for him, not when no one else except Eckhart could do it, but knew we had to try. "

"For a hat?"

"Yes. He was dying."

"Oh."

Petra hadn't told anyone, hadn't wanted to, but the words were unspooling before he could stop them. "He'd tried to fetch the hat himself, but whatever fear was keeping everyone else out kept him out, too. He was old. His heart was strained already, and that night stretched him too thin."

"But you got it for him?"

"Yes." If he closed his eyes, he could still see Iris

stock-still in the doorway, her only trembling in her hands where she gripped the doorframe. They had blamed the early morning for the air too cold to breathe, and Petra had never been as afraid of the dark as he had been for those long minutes. Iris hadn't been able to take one step more, but neither had she turned to leave until Petra reemerged from the dark. "Yes, we got it for him."

"Good."

"When Eckhart came to pay her respects to Nadeen, he told her what I had done. Half the town knew by then anyway, but Eckhart asked if I had seen anything when I was inside, and I said no. After that, she made certain that anyone who wanted anything out of the manor would have to make their plea through her, not me."

"Yes." Fier blinked down at the hands he'd splayed in his lap. "That sounds like something she would do."

"She won't say so, but I know she worries that I might get hurt. She says – everyone says – that there's a monster here."

"I bet they also say that monster is me." Fier curled his fingers closed again, but otherwise held absolutely still. "They'd be right."

Fier

A RISING WIND rattled the window casings and left rain streaked across the glass. From his place on the floor, Fier watched the droplets coalesce and run in rivulets down the pane. If this was a dream, it was a welcome one. Any scene at all was a welcome reprieve from the spinning, starlit dance and the wandering hands.

The flower stood crooked in its jar again, placed there, of course, by Petra. Fier had managed not to flinch when the gardener retrieved it from near his knee, and he'd watched in silence while the plant was adjusted and watered. Petra handled it as if it were glass itself, but even Fier, with his spoonful of botanical knowledge, could tell it was a living thing: all the glass or silk flowers he'd been given by admirers had been grand, full-bloomed beauties, and while the petals on the borders of this one flared outward like slender tongues of fire, those at the center curled inward, clustered protectively over an unseen heart. It was alive and (given its nightly tumbles) resilient, and the gardener need not have handled it so carefully.

As for the gardener himself – how different he was when he knew there were eyes on him. Gentle still, but so stiff and formal. He wore no easy smile or private fondness or anything but sobriety and ill-disguised discomfort. He kept his head tilted, like a wild horse expecting and avoiding a bridle, and Fier regretted the questions that had so set his company on edge.

"You can leave if you want to. I won't keep you." Fier managed to add a smile to the offer – a glass one, perhaps, but a smile nonetheless.

Petra, studying him with a serious cant to his eyebrows and mouth, did not reply. He'd said nothing for these last long minutes, and he said nothing still. He wore a leather cord at his neck, and this he ran between his fingers with the slow, slow steadiness of someone fathoms deep in thought.

"And you can tell Sir Eckhart." Glass smile, glass voice. "There's nothing she can do, but she might as well know I'm here."

"I don't think you're a monster."

Guilt bubbled back up from the pit of Fier's stomach and the prince tipped his gaze up to the ceiling. "You wouldn't—" Glass-voiced again: thin and brittle and breakable. He cleared his throat, tried a second time: "You wouldn't know."

"It's not knowing yet. It's just a feeling."

Just a feeling. What trust could be put in that? For as long as Fier could remember, his body had lied to him in every instance: a *feeling* had led him to lashing out at his dance partners; a *feeling* had led him to snubbing the witch on the doorstep; a *feeling* had led him to attacking Eckhart. Now, caught so often between distress and the choking fear of that lantern-lit courtyard, *feelings* would tear him to pieces from the inside-out.

Petra did not speak again, and Fier glanced at him, caught him studying the now-watered flower with the same seriousness with which he'd studied Fier. All this for a plant. The sunlit visits, the morning greetings, the painfully soft smiles – all for a plant. Fier was the intruder here: an unwanted stranger thrown into another's well-worn routine.

"If you like it so much, you can have it." As Petra turned toward him, confused, Fier tipped his head toward the flower. "Take it."

Petra drew back, startled at last out of his sobriety and into blatant surprise. "Your Grace, that's not-- that's not mine to take."

"It's Fier. And someone probably left it for me, which makes it mine. Now I'm giving it to you, and that makes it yours."

"Fier. You should keep it."

"Well, I don't want it. You like it more than I do. You take care of it. It should be yours. It's already yours."

Far from being reassured, however, Petra looked instead as if he might be sick. Dismay lodged in Fier's throat, set his pulse skittering. Refusing a gift from royalty had, during his short and ineffective reign here, been seen by the townsfolk as nearly an act of treason. The last three years must have been rife with changes if *this* was what happened when Fier offered someone a gift they had actually seemed to want.

"If you don't want to, you don't have to. I mean that. You don't have to."

Petra drew in a long breath through his nose, and Fier watched the distress melt from his face. By the time the gardener finished an equally-long exhale, his expression had regained its previous stoicism. But Petra's inexplicable reaction had left Fier jittery, and the prince twined his hands together so tightly they hurt.

He wanted to ask what he'd done wrong, why a gift of a flower was something so alarming, what the odds were of Petra ever coming back to the manor after this wreck of a conversation. But even with his sobriety reinstated, Petra still sat with his face partially turned away, his shoulders tense and square. As

Fier watched, he tugged at the ends of his sleeves. A shadow like the one on the gardener's face tracing the curve of his wrist – an inborn spill of ink across his skin.

That's what he's doing, Fier realized with a pulse of understanding as Petra pulled the sleeves down as far over his hands as he could. *He's hiding.*

"I want to go for a walk. A walk inside," he amended, as Petra began to turn toward the window, "not out in the rain. Will you come with?"

"Do you want me to?"

"Yes. I wouldn't ask if I didn't."

Petra hesitated (with, Fier noticed, another side-long glance at the impromptu vase and its flower), but voiced no complaint. "Until the rain stops," he ceded, "and then I should go."

Fier expected *something* when he left his bedroom: a dizzy spell or foreboding crawling like a cold breeze across the back of his shoulders. But there was nothing. The only change between one room and the next was the shift in scenery.

With the storm outside reaching them as a distant growl, the two of them wandered out of the room and into the hallway with an arm's span between them and the gardener half a step behind. Though his toes passed without resistance through the piled rugs underfoot, and though his steps fell with an unnatural silence, as he and Petra fell into step together, Fier could almost imagine the steady tread of the gardener's footfalls were his own.

They wandered through hallways and through open sitting rooms, Fier trailing his fingers through armchairs and across the spines of ordered books. He had expected to see the manor reduced to its bones, but as far as he could tell, the furniture sat where it always had, the pottery and spun glass ornaments ranged as always along shelf and mantle and table.

The stillness, truth be told, weighed more heavily than the silence. The absence of the always-bustling staff turned the place into an empty, but not desecrated, tomb.

He felt more than saw Petra's eyes on him instead of their surroundings, and when Fier caught glimpses of him from the corner of his eye, the gardener walked with his shoulders partially hunched, his hands held stiffly at his sides. His expressions, in one form or another, all seemed to consist of frowning by degrees.

"So you come in here to fetch things. And water the flower."

Annoyance – or embarrassment – ghosted across Petra's face. "Yes. I don't take anything that belongs here."

"How do you know what's mine and what isn't?"

"I don't. Eckhart does."

"But no one's come yet for your flower?"

"It's not mine."

"It's not mine, either. Not of it is, really," Fier added, as he passed from hip to knee through an empty table. "I've just been visiting."

"Can you walk through the walls? If I might-- I might ask."

"I don't know. Let's find out."

He could not, as they discovered, walk through walls. Some thin, invisible barrier stopped his hand a fraction from the wood. His feet were the same: he hovered, ghostlike indeed, just above the bare floor.

Petra watched, politely distant, as Fier tried to push his elbow through the wall. Undivided attention from anyone tended to leave the prince queasy, but Petra seemed interested only in the mechanics of the situation (and Fier was safe anyway, without a body), with the unexpected result that Petra's curiosity was almost contagious.

Petra closed a door; Fier put his arm through it. Petra pulled the curtains back from a shrouded window; Fier tried to press his palm against the glass. The stairs down to the second floor proved a mix: the stairs held him up, but Fier could swing his hand through the banister without the least resistance.

The second floor brought with it a tightening in

his chest, as if a hand had closed around his heart and was pulling it back toward the stairs. The draw was insistent, but painless, and as it felt nothing like the stirrings of an impending panic, Fier put it out of his mind.

"We're going to the library," he announced, in answer to a question Petra had not asked. "You can pick where we go after that."

"You have a library?"

Technically the manor did have a library, but Fier, stepping inside, could see why Petra had not thought so. The room had only two floor-to-ceiling bookcases, and most of the room had been given over to a cluster of the same overstuffed armchairs that occupied the rest of the manor. Books ranged along the shelves, yes, but they shared space with brass statuettes and glass trinkets and carved rosewood tokens gifted to the manor's current occupant and those previous.

From their first day of residence, Sir Eckhart had insisted upon this as the site of Fier's lessons, all the long hours of them, but Fier was not there for the scribbled documents on the desk in the corner or the books stacked beside. He headed straight for the armchairs.

There it lay – just where he'd left it. The oblong case sat propped in one of the chairs, the gold flowers inlaid on its lid muted in the rain-shrouded light from the window.

"Can you open this for me?" He didn't turn to see if Petra had followed him into the room, only assumed that he had. "Just for a second."

Petra had, indeed, followed him in, and, without a word, acquiesced. The metal clasp clicked open. Up the lid rose, and inside, undisturbed on its stretch of velvet, as immaculate as the day Fier had set it there, lay the prince's last remaining violin.

As much as his fingers itched to pick it up, to adjust the pegs and rosin the bow, to see the instrument undamaged was almost peace enough. If someone on the night of the curse had crept into his room to leave him a flower, anyone might have snuck in here with theft in mind, but his violin was here, as it would be tomorrow and tomorrow and every day after.

Fier turned with a careful disinterest to his companion. "Can you play?"

"No. I'm sorry."

"That's alright. It's in one piece, at least." Teaching Petra how to play the violin seemed at present to be a less difficult task than getting him to smile. "Let me show you the most boring book in this whole room."

As much as Fier wanted to make a point of walking on Petra's right side, the gardener still kept his head angled, so the prince skirted Petra's left on his way to the nearer of the two bookshelves and crouched to check the spines of the titles lining the lowest shelf.

"Here it is. *The Manual of Practice, Rules of Proceeding, and Debate in Deliberative Assemblies.*" He touched – or attempted to touch – the flaking brown binding. "Really dull. Put me to sleep by page two."

The violin case closed behind him with a click, and Petra crouched beside Fier with more than enough room for another person to sit between them.

"Or this one," Fier went on. "*The First Part of the Common Laws Including Illustrative and Exceptional Cases.* There's a whole chapter devoted to *all* the different ways a person can rent or loan property. In summary, there are far too many. Absolutely riveting."

"Do you want your body back?"

The unexpected question sent a shock of alarm from Fier's chest to his fingertips. Beside him, Petra's mouth was still a thin and serious line, his eyes deep and dark and earnest. Some people had eyes that chased you, pinned you, flattened you; these, though, were eyes you tripped into.

Did he want his body back? No. His stomach lurched so suddenly at the prospect that he felt sick. No. *No.* A violin and the chance to page through books were not temptation enough.

"No." The steadiness of his voice surprised him, and Fier risked a secondary answer before he could waver: "Never."

Petra said nothing to that, and Fier's stomach churned with the cold, watery beginnings of suspicion. Why would Petra want Fier to have his body back? What did Petra intend to get out of Fier having his body back?

No – *no*. Adoring smiles for the garden's flowers, gentleness and patience for the fragile green twists of the newly-grown. Petra would not – *could not* – hurt.

But Fier's throat was tight and his mouth dry as he resumed his tour of the library shelf. "Some of these you might like. *A Catalog of Local Flora*, maybe. It has painted illustrations." He wanted to curl up and draw his hands back to himself, but he ghosted his hand through another worn volume instead. "But you probably know all of the plants here."

Petra slid the book from the shelf and paged through it. The illustrations in question were as bright and clean as Fier remembered, despite their three-year sojourn on the shelf. But, as Petra flipped through the thin selection of flowers, Fier's confidence wavered. Of course the book would be only a fleeting interest: the gardener would prefer the real things to the paintings, and he was surrounded by the real things all day.

"You can take the book with you, if you want," he added anyway. "Or read it here whenever you feel like it."

"It is very pretty," Petra conceded, but he replaced it on the shelf – a polite refusal.

They picked through the shelves, then, but suspicion had lodged itself in Fier's thoughts and scrambled the rest; prickling fear aggravated the still-ceaseless pull at his chest, until the prince gave in and wrapped his arms around his middle, tucked his gloved hands against his ribs to keep them from shaking.

"*A Lecture on the Influences of Medical Advances upon the Law Transcribed.*" Petra touched, so lightly, the crowded gilt letters of the title. "Did you like that one?"

"No. Not much."

The gardener tried again with *A Mathematical Study of the Movements of the Celestial Bodies* and *The Whole Art of the Surveying of Land*, but Fier managed only a shrug at the last, and Petra went back to the catalog of plants, sat on the floor, and riffled through the pages.

"This one," he began, pausing on a page Fier was not quite close enough to see, "is alyssum. When you plant it, you don't bury it in the soil. The seeds need light to grow – they need the sun. Once you get them growing, they flower all summer, and pop up anywhere they can. The white flowers are the most common, and if you let them, they'll cover the whole ground. Like fallen snow."

Fier crouched beside Petra and the book, far enough to be out of reach, but close enough to see the tumble of white and blue flowers across the upturned page. He listened halfway, the rhythm of the speaking voice more valuable than the spoken words.

"This one is chamomile, which is used for tea. It has a strong smell even as a flower, so it keeps insects away from anything you plant nearby. Some people treat it like a weed. These are tulips, which you have on the door to your room. They start out as bulbs, which look a little like potatoes. They grow best when they are cold, so you plant them in autumn. You water them once before they sprout, but only once. And you don't water them much after they sprout, either."

"You could be making all this up and I wouldn't know."

The corner of Petra's mouth crimped upward in the flickered start of a smile. "Then you didn't read this book much."

The worry smoothed out of him – at least enough for his hands to be steady again – and Fier couldn't help the genuine if lopsided smile that stole over his own features. "I know what you're doing."

"Is it working?"

"A bit."

"Are you alright?"

"A bit."

Silence settled, heavier than those before, and Fier did not at once recognize the cause: the rain had lessened and the wind had stopped. The storm's tapping at the window had fallen to a whisper.

Petra must have noticed, too. With an almost apologetic slowness, he closed the book and set it back on the shelf. He and Fier rose together and, at an unspoken agreement, began the winding walk back the way they'd come. Fier said nothing; at his shoulder, neither did Petra. The tension and endless pull in his chest gradually lessened until, as they reached his bedroom, both vanished entirely.

Petra lingered in the doorway as Fier passed through, but Fier caught the glance he cast the flower still upright on the bedside table. Seeing it in the slowly-breaking sunlight loosened something in the gardener's shoulders, but Fier knew better than to offer it as a gift a second time.

"Thank you for visiting." To his ears, the phrase sounded too formal to convey genuine gratitude, but Fier did not know what other words to use. "If you were to visit again, you would be most welcome."

Petra nodded and folded his hands politely behind his back. "I will come back tomorrow."

Surprise hooked his heart into his throat, but Fier ignored it. "To water the flower," he guessed. "Please do."

"That, yes. But also to see you." Brown eyes met his, and the surprise, this time, was not so easily dismissed. "If I may."

Not sure if he should speak, not sure if the lurch in his stomach was due to hope or dread, Fier settled for a nod. Petra returned the gesture, his almost deep enough to be a bow, and stepped back into the hallway, and with two steps more was out of sight. A handful of minutes later, Fier saw him from the window as he crossed the grounds, his footsteps leaving a trail through the dark and rain-soaked grass.

Petra

FROM A DISTANCE, the plants were a forest: rows of tangled green, a wall too dense to see through, growing over and through their wood-and-wire trellises with abandon. Seen closer, the vines tapered into delicate curls, and these hooked around fingers and wrists, jostled as much by the breeze as by the shifting weight of the harvesters in their midst. Someone in another row was singing, but their voice, quiet already, was almost inaudible against the rustle of shifting leaves.

He could hear the murmur of conversation, too, wordless and soothing in the background of his work. The vine-thin stems had grown so tall that Petra could not see over them, and while the tall and narrow rows made some of the townsfolk claustrophobic, Petra liked the privacy. And the peace of Eckhart industrious beside him, dropping her picked pea pods into a shared basket, was a rare gift: a chance to be alone but not lonely, to work in rhythm with someone as comfortable with silence as with words. The rest of the townsfolk stayed two or three rows away, as they always did, and left the two of them in a world of their own.

On any other occasion, the repetitive test and snap and toss of pods would have been meditative. On this morning, as with the afternoon and evening before, Petra's thoughts had yet to stop boiling.

He played it over and over again: *Do you want your body back* and the way Fier froze in response – his whole body suddenly and sharply tense, his prior exuberance shaken and ground into nothing. He had come back, slowly, but if Petra hadn't seen his reaction, hadn't talked until Fier lost his blank stare, would Fier be stuck there still? *Do you want your body back* and Fier had nearly drowned.

A garden spider skittered across a leaf and onto his fingers. Petra paused in his work as it raced up the back of his hand on needle-thin legs. Blocking its ticklish progress along his arm, he coaxed it onto his other hand, and eased it back in among the vines.

"Sir Eckhart?"

"Hmm?"

"What was the prince like?"

The rustle and snap stilled by half as Sir Eckhart paused in her work, but Petra did not slow or look in her direction. Let her think he had asked only out of curiosity. The question meant nothing; the answer meant nothing.

Shifting leaves, a dull *tck* as a pod landed in the wheeled basket between them. If she had been studying him before, she wasn't now. "Prince Fier, you mean?"

"Yes."

"He was kind, once, and full of light. Inquisitive, though most called him impertinent. Clever when he wanted to be. And stubborn, always so stubborn."

Again, a pause. Petra dallied in his search for ripe peas and untucked leaves from where they had been caught between the vines and the support wire. Was this useful? Was this what he'd wanted to hear?

Sir Eckhart, though, had not finished. "The beast is not him," she went on, snapping a pod from its vine with more force than necessary. "No matter what the rest of this town believes, Fier was never a beast. He was hurt and he was unhappy, but at his heart, he was never a beast."

"Never?"

"No. He was something rare." Eckhart's expression clouded, and she let the pod tip from her fingers into the basket. "Something precious."

He's alive. The words rose in his throat. *He's alive, and he's still hurt.*

Was he supposed to tell her? Was he supposed

to keep this a secret? Fier had begged for secrecy, and his eventual relenting had sounded more like resignation than a change of heart. Fier was hurt, and he needed help, but was Eckhart part of what frightened him?

"Petra."

Petra jumped – and knew his reaction was out of place. She would know something was wrong. Uncertainty twisting wild in his stomach, he closed his eyes and bowed forward until his nose and forehead nudged against the leaves and vines and trellis wire already sharp against his hands. He would not speak. This was not his secret to give away.

"He is still alive." Against the backdrop of his closed eyes, Eckhart's voice, smooth and low, rolled through him like a tide. "There may be much I do not understand about magic and about Fier, but I do not and cannot believe that curse was meant to kill him. There is – there must be – a way out. Fier will find it. He is alive. Wherever he is, he is alive. He will come back.

"And when he does, I will be here."

Petra

WHEN PETRA REACHED THE PRINCE'S ROOM, Fier was sitting on the floor in the same place as the previous morning: hands lax, face tilted up toward the window, expression thoughtful. Afternoon sunlight bathed his head and shoulders and threaded his hair with gold.

For a moment, Petra was afraid the day before had never happened. The prince would turn, uncomprehending, and not remember Petra or any of what had been said. But Fier turned and recognition spread across his face in a smile.

"You did come!" Surprise left him glowing. "Good! I want to ask you some things."

Petra lingered in the doorway and watched as, legs folded, Fier spun to face him instead of the window. The smile lingered, but it looked tight – frantically cheerful in a way that suggested something fraying. A mask bright with false paint.

"I have some questions for you, too."

Fier wavered, a rabbit catching an unfamiliar scent, but his eyes were bright even as his smile faded. "We can take turns. You ask first."

In lieu of an immediate reply, Petra skirted Fier in a wide circle to seek then collect the flower from the shadow of the bed. Fier hunched his shoulders and tracked him without blinking, but Petra only took up the flower and the empty jar and placed the one in the other as he sat across from the prince on the rug.

Before he could change his mind, he slid the flower into the space between them. "This," he whispered, mouth dry, "is you."

Petra had expected disbelief, even ridicule, but Fier, to his credit, did not laugh or tease or even crack an irreverent smile. He stared at the flower with the same puzzled focus he'd leveled on Petra the day before, then flicked his gaze up to Petra, searching and serious, and even though Petra's instinct was to look away, he knew better than to do so now.

"That," the prince ventured softly, "is not a question."

"Do you believe me?"

"Maybe. But I don't feel it." Fier waved a hand as if trying to pull more-apt words out of the air. "You pick it up, or it falls down, and I don't feel that. I don't feel anything at all."

Petra had been prepared to convince him along

a different track – the petal's colors, the timing, the weight of magic – and without an effective, planned response, he hesitated. "It's not... it's not your body," he began. "It's *you*."

Fier propped his elbow on his knee, tucked his chin against his hand. His eyes were again on the flower. "What's the difference?"

"It's your soul. Your heart."

"My heart?" Disbelief, now, at last, stole into Fier's voice, and his mouth twitched into a humorless smile. "No. Mine's not something so pretty."

A crack of heat lanced through Petra's chest. "Don't say that," he snapped, then – as Fier looked up at him, startled – said again, with forced calm, "Don't say that."

Fier opened his mouth as if to protest further, but Petra must have done a poor job of concealing his indignation: the prince exhaled in a huff instead. He wrapped his arms around his waist, fingers tight in the fabric of his formal jacket. "Fine. If it *is* me, so what? Leave me as a flower. Better that than a man."

Petra hesitated again, this time for fear of asking what he had, as a near-stranger and as a commoner, no real right to ask. But, "Here," he began, "is my question."

Perhaps catching on to Petra's reluctance, or perhaps out of fear for what might come next, Fier tensed, his nod of acquiescence quick and shallow.

"Did you, before the curse, not want a body?"

"Yes." The prince's voice was brittle but clear. "Almost always."

Petra knew better than to ask why. He could see Fier curling in on himself already, his back curved like a strung bow, his head low, his eyes unblinking. The wrong words would freeze him again, send him adrift again. *What hurt you?* rose to the tip of his tongue, but Petra knew better than to ask that, either.

"So the witch, when she cursed you, gave you what you wanted?"

Fier blinked at that, but his eyes lost none of their wariness. "She did."

"And the nightmares…?"

"Show that I was right to want this. My turn."

Petra sat back with relief sinking through the tumult of his stomach. Fier had not drowned; he had not pushed too far.

With some effort, Fier pulled himself upright. His was a royal posture, his back straight and his hands on his knees, even if he was seated on the floor instead of a throne. A prince holding court on the carpet.

"Who was 'we'?" he asked.

"Pardon?"

"Yesterday you said, 'we tried to get his hat for him,' when you told me about the old gardener. Who was 'we'?"

"Oh." Dark hair curling against her cheeks, green-and-gold eyes fierce and full of mischief. The image brought a sudden stab of grief, no less sharp for the years intervening. "Iris. She was an apprentice with me."

"I never see her outside with you."

"After Nadeen died, she left for the city."

"She was a friend?"

"Yes." Petra stared unseeing at the dirt-encrusted edge of his boot, ignored the growing weight in his chest. "Nearly a sister."

"Could she come in, too? Into the manor after the curse?"

The change in course gave Petra room to push back the rush of homesickness, and his tone was easily smooth as he replied: "No. She took one step inside and had to stop. I went the rest of the way alone."

"So coming here on behalf of someone else is not enough." Fier, adopting an expression of intense thought, dropped his elbows to his knees. "But that's what you do. That's what Eckhart did, if only once."

"Eckhart was attacked. That's no secret." Fier flinched, but Petra continued: "Selflessness wasn't enough. Bravery wasn't enough. Eckhart is braver than anyone, and the beast caught her."

"But it's never caught you?"

"I've not even seen it." Truth be told, Petra would have doubted its existence at all, had Eckhart not been the one to tell him otherwise. "It's never bothered with me."

"Why?"

"I don't know," Petra admitted, but the villagers' guesses caught in the current of his thoughts: *He's beastly, too. The beast is afraid of him. He's a witch, he's a witch, he's a witch.*

Oblivious to this, of course, Fier remained lost in contemplation. "So you can come inside *and* the beast leaves you alone," he mused. "Why are you different?"

For the first time in years, Petra had to resist the urge to touch his face, to hide with his hands what he'd learned to keep out of sight with a tilt of his chin. He twisted sideways, perhaps too late, but Fier, far from scrutinizing him, was staring into the middle distance and seemed to be asking in earnest.

"And what does it *want*?" the prince went on. "Why is it even here?"

"It's part of the curse. Maybe the biggest part."

Fier's attention slid to Petra. "Are you a part of it, too?"

Surprise sent a current of lightning through his bloodstream, but Petra held very still, and with resolve, returned Fier's gaze. Fier asleep until Petra woke him.

84

No one but Petra able to walk through the manor unharmed and (mostly) unafraid.

"Nothing here frightens you. Nothing here hurts you." The prince's green eyes were bright, so bright – alive with thoughts running parallel to Petra's own. "You're the only one."

"That night – the curse – nothing happened to me."

"I was asleep until you. I was in a dream until you. *That* spent three years in the dark," he indicated, with a nod, the flower between them, "and, every day, you put it in the sun. Every day, you pick it up. Every day, you move it. You are changing things. You are breaking the rules."

"I am not going to break your curse," Petra insisted, alarmed at, but unable to temper, the vehemence in his own voice. "I wouldn't even try. How could I? You don't want it broken."

Fier had left off blinking again. His face was masked by the same careful blankness of the day before. "Do *you* want it broken?" he asked, speaking with a deceptive lightness.

He's afraid. Petra's heart constricted in his chest. What could he say? *Trust me* would mean nothing; *I'm not going to hurt you* would mean nothing.

"Fier," he began, as careful as possible, as gentle as possible, "this is your place, and you have every right to ask me to leave. If you want me to go, then I will go. If you don't want me to come back, then I will not—"

But he broke off as Fier closed his eyes and jerked his head in abrupt refusal. He raked his hands through his hair, left them buried there – and stayed like that for so long that Petra began to worry that he ought to leave anyway, if only to give Fier a chance to recover in private.

With a long, bracing breath, Fier relaxed his shoulders and dropped his hands back into his lap. He kept his eyes closed, loosely so, and regained the upright, princely bearing he'd adopted before.

"You won't break it." He sounded as if he was attempting to convince himself as much as Petra. "You won't break it."

With so much of Fier's peace of mind at stake, *I'll try not to* seemed a shallow reply, but a promise was more than Petra could give. Without knowing the nature of the knot, how could he promise not to un-ravel it, even by accident? Removing himself entirely was the only way to guarantee that he could not and would not have an effect.

"I *will* leave if you want me to, Fier."

Fier shook his head again, his eyes resolutely closed. "I want you to visit."

"Okay."

"No more questions today."

"Okay."

"Good." With the matter so settled, Fier opened his eyes at last and clapped his hands together. "Done. Are you hungry?"

Petra hesitated, but when Fier's expression did not shift from one of frank concern, he replied: "No, thank you."

"That's good. There's nothing here to eat, anyway. Let's explore again. You choose where."

Fier's cheer rang false: too bright, too fast, too scrambled to be genuine. Now that he knew to look for it, Petra could see the mask slipping back into place, but the mask was a shield, too, and Petra would not break that any more than he would break anything else.

"If I choose, then I choose outside."

Though vigilant for any shift in Fier's poise, Petra need not have paid such close attention: Fier's shoulders hunched as if against a sudden draft.

"Or," Petra amended, "the sun room."

"The...? The solarium? Lead on, then."

This time, Petra took the glass jar with him into the corridor. Fier did not protest, though he did cast the flower another skeptical glance as he fell in step at Petra's left shoulder.

"If that isn't me," he mused, "you're making a lot of fuss over a flower."

"It *is* you," Petra insisted, with a sharper tone than intended. "And your heart makes a very pretty flower, whether you like it or not."

"What do you think yours would look like?"

Petra's heart lurched into his throat. *Brambles, maybe,* was his instinctive response. With difficulty, he managed instead, "I believe that's a question."

Fier's mouth twisted into a comically exaggerated frown, and Petra, pushing off his momentary dismay, fought a smile.

Theirs was a shorter walk than before, with none of the investigations of the day previous and no need to travel far. Mercifully short, in fact, as Petra did not know what to say or how to artfully speak of nothing, and Fier kept pace with his lips pressed tightly together, as though afraid another question might slip out.

Stepping into the solarium was, in a way, like stepping outside. Undiluted afternoon sunlight streamed into the room through great glass panes on the walls and ceiling, the brightness of it and the warmth of it painting the window seats and faded wooden floor in bands of gold. The corridor, and even the prince's room, had been so shaded by comparison that Petra halted in the doorway, blinking back tears as his eyes adjusted.

The solarium had once teemed with plants –

great-leafed ferns and trailing strands of pink and red flowers with the smooth and delicate lines of blown glass – but gardeners had called back their gifts, one after the other, until the ample sunlight poured over bare walls and empty shelves. The room was, altogether, a shallow replacement for the verdant safety of the gardens, but the sun was welcome, and Petra felt the best of it burrow into his heart.

Fier ghosted partway across the threshold, then likewise paused. If the sun's radiance stung his eyes, he gave no sign, but he lifted his chin with a sigh and a curl to his mouth that might have been the beginnings of a smile.

"I can feel *that*," he whispered.

Petra watched the black-gloved hands uncurl and led the way into the room proper. Fier trailed behind, his eyes half-closed as if nearly drowsing.

Mindful of the jar in his hands and its long-stemmed occupant, Petra settled himself cross-legged on the floor with the jar cradled in his lap. Fier took a seat on his left (within arm's reach, this time, if only just) and, with a deep, sleepy sigh, lost the tension in his shoulders.

Know where you are, Nadeen had been fond of saying. *Your feet are on the ground. You are here.* And *here* was in the sun, wearing the heat of it like a second skin, the wood of the window seat behind him unyielding against his spine, the wood floor beneath him smooth and still cool, the glass in his hands fragile despite its weight.

Tomorrow, he might accidentally untangle the curse beyond repair. Tomorrow, he might send Fier tumbling back into the panic that had caught him in the library. Tomorrow, he might overstay his welcome at last.

But for now, they sat side by side in untroubled silence. Fier had not wanted him to leave. Fier had smiled upon seeing him – even, faintly, smiled now – and Fier did not want him to leave.

With a final glance at the prince to make sure his eyes were still firmly shut, Petra, too, tilted his head back and closed his eyes and soaked in the warmth of the late-spring sun.

Fier

FOR THE FIRST TIME IN MEMORY, Fier did not dread the dawn of new days.

Every morning, he woke, shivering from tangled nightmares, his room lightless in the grey before sunrise, and curled in on himself in the corner until the shaking stopped and he could remember, through the haze of skittering panic, how to breathe.

But every morning, too, he *woke*. The sun burned off the fog of sleep and the echo of creeping hands, and Fier knew with a rich, solid certainty – stronger each day – that this was not a dream. He was alive. He was awake.

Thus awake, he could see, now, what so often knocked the flower from its impromptu vase. Each night, when the sun withdrew the last of its rays from his room, Fier retreated to the corner, and each night, a shadow detached from any host crept beneath his bedroom door and stole across the carpet toward the bedside table.

Sometimes the shadow was shapeless – an amorphous puddle of starless night pooling into his room. Sometimes it stood on two legs and staggered across the rug with its feet loose and melting and un-formed. Its head – when it had one at all – had no eyes or mouth or nose; too-large, it tilted wildly, jostled by its erratic movements, and more often than not hung loose on its neck.

Each night, Fier watched from his hiding place in the corner, holding his breath to escape its notice as it curled up the legs of the table or hunched a half-formed body over the small and fragile glass jar. With a hand or body or melting black mass, the shadow stole over the flower, and, as always—

Stars. He had never seen so many stars.

But the nightmarish visit and the torturing dream that followed were a terror to face only when the sun went down. In the long stretch of time be-tween waking and dreaming, Fier could push the shadow to the back of his mind and pretend that its existence was a problem for a later time, a later Fier.

And while the nights may have been hellish, the days were well worth the fear.

True, he may have been too frightened to visit any of the other rooms on his own, but he could sit on the rug in his bedroom and watch the room slowly fill with light, or he could watch the rain streaking against the windows or the clouds skating with regal slowness across the sky.

Whenever possible, though, he watched Petra.

No one, surely, could be so unfailingly careful, but the gardener, seemingly, was careful with everything. With the newly-sprouted, certainly, but with the old growth, too: with a feather-light hand, he touched the rough bark of trees in polite greeting or nudged aside curtains of slender willow branches when he passed beneath. Sometimes, when he knelt chest-deep in flowers, he would rock back, hand tilted, and Fier could just make out the jewel-bright beetles trickling across his fingers. The gardener placed them on flowers well out of the way of his work. He did the same with earthworms: after any amount of rain, they sprawled across the garden's stone paths, and with each one he came across, their keeper conscientiously relocated them to the flowerbeds.

With a sharpness so frequent it hurt, Fier wanted to see *more*. He wanted to see Petra with Eckhart, to see how they got along; he wanted to see Petra with the villagers, who surely adored him for his kindness and his hard work; he wanted to see Petra with his now-absent family: Who had he been with Iris? Who had he been with Nadeen? Who had he been with the pair of them? Had he grown up with them? What had he been like before meeting them?

Fier had wanted, too, obscurely, to see Petra asleep, and this, at least, had been a wish granted: on one soft summer afternoon, he had seen the gardener resting against one of the trees, his eyes closed and his hands folded in his lap. The sun through the leaves overhead speckled his face and shoulders with shifting light and shadow. Butterflies and bees looped harmlessly around him and settled sometimes in his hair or on his arms. He had rolled back the green sleeves of his shirt, and Fier could see the spill of inborn ink curling past his wrists all the way up to his elbow and, presumably, onto the canvas of skin beyond.

As reliable as the sunrise, Petra visited every day, usually late into the morning, and Fier took to watching for him out of the window and, at his approach, waiting for him just inside the doorway of his bedroom. While Petra did not smile upon seeing him, Fier could no more hide his own delight than he could stop the skip of his heartbeat, even as he held himself well out of arm's reach.

"Did you sleep well? Did you have a good morning? Were you busy?" The questions bubbled out of Fier as fast as thought, and even though he had, at first, clapped his hands over his mouth to stifle his never-welcome curiosity, Petra answered them politely, both on the first day asked and on every day since

– a patience and thoughtfulness Fier was so grateful for, he might have wept. He wanted to ask and ask and ask – for the banalities, for the details, for everything – but Petra answered the small morning questions with obvious stiffness, and seemed to prefer silence, and so Fier bit back his impertinence.

When he was on his own, the manor seemed far too empty and imposing to explore, but in Petra's company, Fier would have ventured anywhere, from the attic to the cellars. No shadow frightened Petra, and so no shadow frightened Fier. At his choice, they wandered together up the narrow attic stairs and investigated furniture shrouded in white sheets, everything layered in a dust older than the curse; they wandered to the lowest levels of the manor, into the pantry and wine cellars, every shelf and corner empty.

Petra often chose the solarium, and soon that was their most frequent destination, the afternoons there often full of rich, honeyed sunlight. On the stormy days, of which summer promised many, they sat side by side and watched the rain sheeting past the windows and the lightning arc against the rumbling sky. On those days, though Fier felt no downward shift in temperature, Petra borrowed a blanket from Fier's room to cocoon himself in, the flower in its glass jar sheltered in his lap.

As warm and sleepy as he felt on the sunnier

days, Fier enjoyed the rainy ones best. He had never expected to feel safe or cozy in the manor, but between the sweeping view of the tumultuous storms and Petra peaceful at his shoulder, Fier could easily believe the house a haven.

Those days loosened his resolve most, and on one particularly harsh day, with the wind rattling the glass and the rain so dense they couldn't see the grounds beyond, Fier brought up the one question he should have asked on the first day:

"How is Sir Eckhart?"

Petra glanced at him, but Fier pretended not to notice. Such scrutiny was only fair, given how often Fier watched Petra unobserved, but Petra's was by far the more-perceptive eye – dangerously so.

"She misses you. She believes in you."

"Not-- no, I mean… Is she happy?"

Petra returned to his study of the rain beyond the window. His reply, this time, was longer in coming. "I don't know. She keeps herself busy. She's made this place her home." He hesitated, openly uncertain, then added, "She is very reserved."

"She wasn't always." Fier lay back, arms crossed over his stomach, and watched the rain patter against the panes set in the ceiling. "When I first met her, she always had little gifts for me in her pockets – usually candied fruit, but sometimes sheets of new music. She snuck them to me between lessons. She's always been formal, but she had softer edges then."

"You miss her." Petra's voice was soft, hardly louder than the clatter of the rain.

"We parted on… poor terms." The whole of the truth stuck in Fier's throat. "I regret that."

"I think she would forgive you. I think she already has."

Guilt rose in a hot, unpleasant tide from his stomach to his throat, and Fier blinked against a prickling at the back of his eyes. "That sounds like her."

"How long have you known her?"

"Since I was seven."

Petra remained still and silent, evidently expecting something more, but Fier did not trust his voice, and he did not want to talk about any of the last fourteen years. He could see Eckhart on the inside of his closed eyelids: twenty years old, barely a knight but already the most regal person Fier had ever met. She was awkward with children and had not been quite sure what to do with her new, excitable charge. Fier loved her on the spot.

When he finally realized there would be no elaboration, Petra, too, lay down. Fier caught him out of the corner of his eye: the profile of his face and the serious line of his mouth; he pulled absently at his sleeves, though they already covered most of ink-touched hands.

"Does it hurt?"

"Does what hurt?" Petra turned to look at him, his eyes dark and deep, and a flicker of lightning lit the smudge on the right side of his face. Fier touched his own cheek in answer, and Petra's expression clouded.

"No." Again, his voice was almost too soft to hear over the storm. "It doesn't hurt."

"You're beautiful, you know. On both sides."

Petra shifted to face the ceiling, then, but after only a second, he drew in a halting breath and hid his face in his hands.

"It's true," Fier insisted, but pushed no further than that. He watched the rain and roiling clouds. When Petra still said nothing, Fier took to counting the streaks of lightning to pass the time. Eckhart had told him stories of fire-breathing dragons, but Fier had always thought fire ill-suited to them. You could tame fire, keep it docile in hearth or candle, but there was no taming lightning. The wild, ragged forks of it; the blinding cracks in the sky – *that* was the stuff of dragons.

He was so lost in thought that he almost missed Petra's eventual reply, but he heard it, still soft, in the wake of a rumble of thunder: "Nadeen found me when I was three."

Fier kept silent, not sure what to say, but Petra continued without prompting:

"He said he found me among the flowers when he was planting seeds for spring. Someone must have left me there, but Nadeen swears no one in town was expecting a baby. He said I was born from the earth, and that's… that's why I have the… the marks."

"Do you believe him?"

"I don't know. He told Iris and the rest of the town that I was his nephew." A pause, just longer than the space of an indrawn breath, and then, as if the previous confession had been a preamble for the real one, Petra spoke again, measured and calm: "I make the flowers grow. I can plant dead seeds and still they sprout. Anything I look after grows bigger and stronger than all the rest. The town thinks I'm a witch. They're afraid of me."

Petra fell silent, then, and the silence was a waiting one, a hungry one. Fier watched the lightning flicker against the clouds and considered this.

"I want to know you better," he decided, "and that doesn't change if you are a witch."

Petra, Fier could see, had returned to toying with the ends of his sleeves, his eyes on the rain above, but his gaze distant. "Are you afraid?"

The back of Fier's neck prickled, and he tucked

his elbows in tight against his sides, twisted his fingers together at his collar. "Not of magic," he admitted, just above a whisper.

"But of me?"

And Petra's eyes were on him again – warm and kind and concerned – and a surge of guilt and sorrow flooded Fier's chest and rose in his throat. "I don't--" Fier broke off, cleared his throat, tried again: "I don't mean to be."

"It's okay if you are." Petra's hands were still now, folded over his ribs. The flower in its jar sat, just visible, at his hip. "It's okay, Fier."

Of course he was afraid. He could feel the shadow of fingers on his neck; he could feel panic coiling in the pit of his stomach – volcanic and fierce and dangerous. Fier had been wrong – over and over, he had been wrong, always wrong – and the chance of being wrong again left him cold.

How easily he could have told Petra everything. In the dark, in the safest place he could think of, protected from the rain and the wind and all the rest of the raging storm, with Petra quiet and attentive, Fier could have pushed away the lump in his throat and confessed to the nightmares, the night of the curse, to seeing everyone around him grow up and grow wild.

But the end of that conversation loomed like the edge of a seaside cliff, and Fier did not want, again, that sickening jolt of once-steady ground tilting underfoot. His family had not believed him, his peers had not believed him, Eckhart had not believed him, and Fier could not have borne that disbelief from Petra.

"Fier." Petra's voice called him back to the present, and before he closed his eyes, Fier saw him pulling himself up into a sitting position. "What do you need?"

"I like your company." Against all odds, Fier managed to keep voice steady. "I don't want to lose that."

"I'm not going anywhere. Not unless you want me to."

"I like your visits."

"Then I will visit."

"I like *you*. And you *are* beautiful." He opened his eyes in time to see Petra blink down at him, startled. "I mean it."

Petra stared at him, apparently at a loss for a reply, and Fier levered himself upright, watching, waiting. Petra's thoughts were impossible to decipher, concealed as they so often were behind the gardener's ubiquitous frown.

"Where do you go when you're not in your garden or in here with me? What do you do?"

The question, like the admission before it, caught Petra off-guard: the crease between his eyebrows deepened and he studied Fier as if he suspected, for once, hidden thorns in the question. But Fier wanted to know, was sick with the need to know the minutiae, and he asked again, with a more casual, if feigned, levity this time: "What sort of life do I borrow my gardener from each day?"

"I help with the harvest." Petra's reply, like so many before, unraveled gradually. "Sometimes the townsfolk ask me to work with plants or animals that are sick or dying, so I do. Or I help with their gardens."

"You help them?" Fier knew he could not keep the confusion from his face or from his voice. "Even though they are afraid of you?"

"Yes."

"Why?"

Petra hesitated, likewise confused. "Because they need help."

Fier considered this. Give everything, expect nothing back. That seemed a dangerous, selfless way to live. Did they know, the townsfolk, what a gift they had in their gardener?

"I was right." Even without the aid of sunlight, Fier felt warm all through. "You are a beauty, and a rare one besides."

Petra held himself absolutely still for a moment, as if intending to speak further, then sat back with nothing more than a small sigh of resignation, and

slid his gaze back to the great glass windows, and after a minute more of silent study, Fier turned to look
with him.

Petra

IN THE FIRST HOUR AFTER SUNRISE, the air was still sharp to breathe and the dew was ice-cold against Petra's bare fingers. The sun was warm on the back of his neck, but not yet strong enough to prompt the removal of his barn coat, and so he paused over and again to pull down the fraying, too-short sleeves.

Ranged up and down the row of raspberry bushes, most crouched as he was, pockets of townsfolk sifted through leaves and thorns in search of ripe berries. Wide, shallow baskets sat in the grass beside each harvester, most of the contents a bright carmine red, but the bushes ran wild, and other baskets, Petra knew, would be swirled with gold or amber or dusty pink. When the small baskets were full, their contents were dumped into the large, half-lidded baskets left at intervals, and the contents of these were marbled gold and rose.

The bushes rambled along the hillsides at chest-height, pushed back only when they encroached on orchards or fields so that they ran in uneven lines, unofficial borders that turned the outskirts of the town into a mosaic.

While harvesting peas had been a morning of quiet industry, shouts and wild singing and raucous laughter cut through the otherwise-still morning air. The youngest of the townsfolk tore up and down the rambling rows, sometimes carrying full baskets for delivery, more often running simply for the joy of running. Most of them were barefoot and sleeveless, sailing past too quickly to identify.

One careened out of a gap in the hedge and tripped— and Petra only just managed to catch her basket as it halfway tipped out of the girl's hands. Raspberries tumbled to the grass like drops of paint. A flicker of movement in the basket, black against bright, caught his eye.

"Thank you!" The girl regained her balance, recognized him, and startled to attention. "I-- I mean, thank you, sir."

This one, with her windswept cloud of dark curls, Petra knew was Asa's little sister, but only as she set her basket on the grass and bent, breathless, to collect the scattered berries could he recall her name: "Maria."

"Yes, sir?"

"Have you been checking these?"

"Checking them?" Maria's half-hearted defer-
ence caved at once to puzzlement. "Checking them for
what?"

"Beetles."

"*Beetles?*"

"Yes, look." With thumb and forefinger, Petra
plucked one of the raspberries out of the basket. Dislodged by the motion, a tiny black beetle crawled out
of the cup of the berry and across Petra's wrist.
"These eat the over-ripe ones from the inside out. We
don't want to collect them with the fruit."

Maria, however, did not seem to be listening.
With the flat of her palm, she cornered the beetle on
Petra's arm and, as it began to crawl up this new ob-
stacle, caught it in the closed bowl of her two hands.

"There's more of these?" she asked. "In the berries?"

"Yes."

A smile of pure, undiluted delight stole over the
girl's face. "Can I keep this one?"

"That's... well, you can try."

Maria continued to beam, and Petra realized,
gradually, that the smile was as much for him as for
the discovery of beetles. Not sure what else to do, he
cast about for something else to say and settled, at a
loss, on, "Are your feet cold?"

"They were, but I can't feel them now. I like

your coat."

"Oh." Involuntarily, Petra glanced down at the mentioned coat. The elbows had been patched, and most of the buttons were missing. "Thank you."

"I'm going to show Asa this beetle now."

Whatever Petra might have said in reply mattered little: Maria had whipped back through the gap in the hedge and was lost to sight. Petra could hear her shouting as she ran back across the field: "Asa! Asa, look at what I found!"

She had forgotten her basket. Petra smiled to himself and began to pick up the rest of the scattered berries, checking each one for insects before replacing them in the basket.

Partway through this process, he chanced to look up— and found that the elderly couple working nearest him had paused in their work to watch him at his. Both of the women had wrinkles etched deeply into their brown, weathered skin; the nearer of the two looked thoughtful, the other astonished, and Petra, flushed with sudden embarrassment, could not understand why.

He ducked his head and hiked up the collar of his coat, but too late: the nearer woman had caught him staring back. With his head still bowed, Petra could hear her creak to her feet and plod across the grass toward him.

Her boots swung to a stop next to his basket. "Here – take this." A canvas coat, faded and softened with age, appeared in his peripheral vision: the woman had shrugged out of her own. "It'll fit you better across the shoulders."

Petra did not reach for it. The townsfolk left food and clothing at his doorstep, never in gifts passed from hand-to-hand.

But the woman did not retract her offered coat, and so Petra reached up for a tentative hold on the jacket's sleeve, painfully aware of how much he had outgrown his own.

"Thank you," he whispered, as, instead of simply letting go, the woman folded the coat over his partially-outstretched arm. "But I haven't... I haven't done anything."

Without looking at her, he could not see her expression, but the sound she made in the back of her throat sounded sad, not scornful. A weight settled on top of his head: her hand on his hair, as light as a bird.

"Take it," she insisted. "You'll grow into it. And if you ever want for food, child, come to us and we'll see you fed."

He should have thanked her again, of course, but was that enough? Was brief and easy gratitude all that was expected from him? He did not want this generosity, did not know what to do with it, and could not understand why it was being offered.

"The tree you planted for us has grown three feet since last summer," the woman continued, her voice soft and mild, as if she recognized Petra's confusion. "Thank you again."

Before Petra could reply, or could even decide how to reply, she removed her hand from his head and returned to her partner, leaving Petra with a new coat and a still-hammering heart.

Petra

FOR THE NEXT FEW DAYS, the full force of the summer sun streamed in through the wide glass windows and turned the solarium into an oven. The rest of the manor retained its unseasonable chill, and its two occupants spent their afternoons roaming the corridors in search of another, more comfortable haven. Fier had recently taken to walking with an energetic, almost bouncing, step, and he had to keep doubling back to wait for Petra, who always walked slowly when he held the jar and its flower in his hands.

They had skirted the library since the beginning, but when the rest of the manor had been seen and seen again, Fier led the way back to the scene of that first visit, and they settled shoulder-to-shoulder on the rug, *A Catalog of Local Flora* open between them, long bars of sunlight washing over the wooden floor and the painted pages at their fingertips.

Petra, of course, knew the book's contents by

heart, and he turned the pages slowly for Fier's bene-fit. The prince lay with his chin propped in his hands, his left elbow a casual handspan from Petra's right.

"I like that one," he mused, pointing at the cur-rent illustration with a finger that passed through the page. "The orchids."

"You've liked all of them so far."

"Yes. And," he added, as Petra turned the page again, "I like those, too."

"The lilies."

"Especially the ones with freckles."

"They look a little like yours," Petra replied, in-dicating with a nod the flower in its modest vase rest-ing on the other side of the book. The flower had turned copper in the sun, its long, flaring petals as full of life and color as when Petra had first seen it. But where the innermost petals had initially been curled inward, some of them now unfurled like the rest, and these few were flecked with gold.

"Not many freckles on mine, though," Fier re-plied, sparing much less attention for the flower. "A lot of the flowers outside aren't in here at all. What are the ones with a brown disk in the center and all those little yellow petals?"

"The sunflowers?"

"Maybe. The bees like them."

"So do I."

111

Petra turned another page, beginning a section on flowering fruit trees. Fier did not comment on these, nor on the vegetables that followed. As they passed the page on sweet potatoes, Petra began to think that Fier's interest had waned, but no sooner had the thought crossed his mind than Fier touched (or attempted to touch) the newest illustration.

"This one. I like this one best." Certainty bolstered the prince's voice, and he spoke in the same candid, almost formal tone with which he had called Petra beautiful, and Petra, looking at the new page, felt his chest constrict as tightly as it had before.

There were no flowers on this page, only a swath of glossy green leaves with the peaked oval shape of so many other leaves on so many other plants. A few of those painted here were untouched, and some were lightly flecked, but most were mottled with irregular splashes of pink, as if the artist had knocked a jar of paint onto his work and then not bothered to fix it. Even so, despite the haphazard look, the blotches of rosy pigment speckled the green with no pattern or symmetry, deliberately so, and each leaf was a strange, separate, marbled work of art.

You're beautiful, you know. On both sides.

Petra could feel the heat rise in his face, and he could feel Fier's eyes on him, and he regretted at once his oversight in letting the prince place himself at his right shoulder.

"You don't have to say that," he whispered.

"Say what?"

The compliment was too much to repeat. "You don't have to lie."

"Lie?" The dismay in Fier's voice kicked Petra's heart into his throat. "It's true! Why shouldn't it be true?"

The sincerity, somehow, was harder to bear than the possibility of empty flattery, and Petra kept his head down, his eyes down, and waited for his heart to unstick itself from his throat.

"Petra, listen." Fier's voice dropped to a murmur, and Petra grit his teeth against the new pressure behind his eyes. "I'll tell you every day until you believe me."

"Tell me what, exactly?"

"That-- What's your favorite flower?"

Petra eyed him, puzzled by the new question, but Fier looked back at him, waiting, bright green eyes unblinking, so he answered: "Alyssum."

"See?" Fier spread his hands as if that solved all. "Roses were my mother's. *I* think roses are plain and have too many thorns, but she loved them. Tulips were my father's – and my eldest sister would pick dahlias."

"And you?"

Fier waved away the question. "The point is, everyone would say their favorite is the best and the most beautiful, but what my mother would consider beauty is not what my father would consider beauty. A flower doesn't have to be a rose to be beautiful, and people who can't see that get stuck with roses and nothing better.

"And I've been surrounded by roses since the day I was born, so trust me when I say that you are by far the most beautiful flower I have ever had the honor to meet.

"So," Fier concluded, clapping his hands together and turning back to the book open between them, "Petra is beautiful, and if he wants me to, I will tell him so every day."

He returned to perusing the book with a surfeit of focus, and Petra twisted together his hands, his mottled hands, and felt again the shadow of the urge to pull down his sleeves and to cover his face until he faded, gradually invisible, into the background.

Beside him, Fier continued to study the painted illustration, evidently content to look at it for as long as it took Petra to turn the page.

Rude, ill-tempered, flighty, capricious. Day by day, year by year, the town's complaints against Fier had accumulated like snow: a light, infrequent drift of flakes that shifted into a blizzard heavy and cold and implacable. On that final morning, Petra had heard one of the kitchen staff complaining to Nadeen over a basket of the season's last apples: "He stuffed a letter from his mother into his cup of tea just to keep Sir Eckhart from reading it. Spilled tea across the table and smudged the ink and burned his fingers, too. How she has put up with him for all these years, I'll never know, but he's not worth this much trouble."

How could *that* Fier be this one? *This* Fier gave voice to disconcerting, heartfelt compliments as easily as if commenting on the weather. *This* Fier wavered toward tears far more often than anger, frightened so easily of Petra knew not what. *This* Fier was fond of the sun and of painted flowers and of *Petra*, and he waited every day just inside the doorway of his bed-room in anticipation of Petra's arrival, balanced on his toes and wearing the most delighted smile Petra had ever seen on a human face.

Beside him, his chin propped in his hands, ap-parently unconscious of his contradictory reputation, Fier still studied the open book. Petra could hear him humming softly under his breath; he knew too little about music to recognize the tune, but his thoughts turned toward the case on the armchair behind them and the prince's obvious longing as he'd gazed upon its contents.

"You could teach me."

"Teach you?" Fier tipped his head, eyes still on the open book. "Teach you what?"

"How to play the violin."

He had the prince's full attention, then: gleaming green eyes fixed unblinking on his, surprise visible in the tense lines of his shoulders. After only a heartbeat of consideration, Fier's mouth cracked into a hopeful smile. "I have an even better idea."

- - -

High-ceilinged and empty, the ballroom felt more like a cave than a proper room. The only windows were slits near the ceiling, and though these allowed strips of summer light to streak the still-polished floor, Petra still shivered as they stepped inside. He never lingered here, but he had noticed in passing the room's only furniture: a four-legged instrument built from dark, glossy wood with a row of grey and off-white at its edge. A bench, likewise four-legged and made of the same polished wood, sat empty at its nearest side.

"This is a piano," Fier explained as they crossed the dance floor. "A visiting diplomat gave it to me as a birthday present when I was seven. I had to beg for weeks for my parents to send it here with me; Eckhart was the one who finally convinced them.

"First, we sit."

As directed, Petra sat at the bench and set the

flower near his feet to keep it out of the way.

On his left, Fier glared at the bench. "*You* will sit," he corrected and, still eyeing the bench, stepped through it. Leaning forward over the piano, he positioned his gloved hands, each finger poised over a different strip of grey or white. "Set your hands like this – on different keys, not mine. The ones in front of you."

Vividly aware of the dirt beneath his fingernails, Petra copied the pose: palms and fingers relaxed. The keys felt smooth and cool against his fingertips, like stone or polished bone.

"Now," Fier's voice had dropped to a whisper, "do what I do."

The prince slid his right hand sideways and his ring finger passed through its new key. Petra followed suit, his movements less smooth, and likewise pressed down. His finger, being solid, depressed the key, and the sound echoed through the wide, empty room, the note cleaner and richer than a bell, bright and pure, snow given sound.

Fier drew in a deep breath and let it out slowly, and Petra would have risked a glance at him had the prince's hands not been shifting again, giving Petra no time to look away.

Fier's hands skated across the keys with an ease that spoke of much practice, and Petra followed in his wake, his touch so light that he might have had no more substance than the prince. He tried not to halt between each note, but to follow Fier's more fluid movement from key to key, filling the empty room with one note at a time, then two, then a stumbling melody as Fier slowed to accommodate the player and as Petra began to understand the shape of the intended music, even if he could not yet match the pace.

Fier's right hand ghosted through Petra's left on its way to new keys, but the prince seemed not to notice, intent as he was on the music, and Petra said nothing, only tried to mirror the change, tried to keep his fingers from tripping over the notes.

Petra had always known music to revolve around singing. Strings or drums could fill the gaps, but voices had always taken the foreground: workers singing in the gardens to pass the time, parents singing in the home to ease their children into sleep, everyone singing in the town square to welcome in a new season or bid farewell to an old one.

The piano unaccompanied sounded lonely, achingly so. Fier may have thought so, too: as his hands stilled, so did Petra's, and thusly finished, the prince quickly swept at his eyes with a sleeve.

"One more time." The words were a plea, and Petra would not have dreamt of refusing.

They started again, resettled fingertips on or just

above the keys, and away went Fier's hands across the grey and white with Petra half a note behind. They knew the rhythm now, knew the unsteady give and take of teaching and learning, and the ringing notes were less halting, less lonely as each followed more easily after the one before. Fier was humming the melody again, half-singing, and while his voice was too quiet to echo, the sound warmed Petra to the tips of his fingers as the piano alone had not.

This time, when they finished, as the last of the music was absorbed into the silence around them, Fier left his hands at the keys, gazing down at them with a soft, reverent smile. With a tiny, private smile of his own, Petra folded his hands in his lap, if only to better the illusion that Fier had been the one playing.

"Thank you." Fier turned to Petra – and his smile did not fade but brightened. "I saw that!"

"Saw what?"

"That smile – blink and you miss it."

Fier's open joy was too contagious for Petra to feel self-conscious, and he could feel another grin pulling inexorably at the corner of his mouth. "I'll play better tomorrow."

"I liked your playing today." Fier cast one last, loving glance at the piano. "I forgot how much I missed this."

Still warm to his fingertips, the promise came

easily: "We can come back tomorrow, if you want. Tomorrow and any day after."

"I would like that," Fier replied, and his melted green gaze shifted again to Petra, who lost, just for a moment, the thread of his thoughts. "Thank you."

Fier

STARS. Fier had never seen so many stars.

He had been here before. He had always never seen so many stars.

He was so sick of stars.

He took in the rest of the scene with a glance, sick, too, of the unchanging scene that met his eye: barren lawns; a rich cascade of gowns and cloaks; jewels and beads gleaming like far-distant suns in hair and across shoulders in great, sparkling strands.

"I've been here before."

"You have, Your Grace."

She wore her leonine mask still, the copper edges of its curling mane gleaming like an unsheathed knife. Her hand in his still gentle – always so, at the start. A light touch: contained, controlled – a formality.

Soft colors in every shade of cream and burnt umber glowed warm in the light, and the swirl of dancers populated the empty gardens like a whirl of autumn leaves. Some caught and nestled against the lantern-strung arbors, hands entwined and heads bent low in secret conversation.

His partner spun, and he turned to follow her step, and the manor stood like a dark and brooding sentinel beyond the proceedings. A light flickered in its uppermost window.

"Eyes on me, prince."

"This is a dream."

"This isn't a dream."

"What is it, then?"

The hand in his tightened; the hand on his shoulder crept toward his neck, and Fier froze. Fear sank cold and jagged into his chest, clawed up his throat, left his heart staggering.

Not all hands.

The careful lift of earthworms from stone paths. A wrist tilted for the blue-green beetle exploring the crevice of a palm. The cradling of the clouded glass jar that carried his heart. Not all hands.

His partner laughed, the sound as sharp as the edges of her mask. "Gentlemen are just as cruel as the ladies, Your Grace. He will be no different."

"Not this one. He won't be like you."

"He will. They always are."

Fier held his tongue. *Not Petra.*

"You have been hopeful before, and you have been wrong. You have always been wrong. You will *always* be wrong."

But against the background wail of the violins, he could hear a piano's halting, half-familiar notes. *Not Petra. Not Petra. Not Petra.*

Another laugh, her hand a vice around his own. He could feel her groping toward his collar, and he hiked his shoulders, tried to wrench his hand free with a strangled "Stop this."

"Get used to this, Your Grace."

"*Stop.* Let me *go.*"

Her hands against his skin, against his wrist. He fought against her hand with both of his, dug at the iron of her fingers, his protests unstoppable, rising to a shout, but he could not get free, he couldn't, and he had to wake up, he *had* to wake up, this was all a dream, and he screwed his eyes shut but not soon enough and she would not let go she would never let go--

Fier snapped his eyes open onto predawn grey. His bedroom – sideways. He lay curled beneath and partway through his bed. The flower and its jar lay on the rug in front of him, tumbled as always from the bedside table above.

He could feel her hand still locked around his, and he massaged his palm, tried to work the shadow of her touch out of his skin, but it lingered still, against his hand and his chest and the back of his neck. Not even the absence of a corporeal body could free him from that.

With nothing to do, then, but wait for morning proper, Fier curled in on himself, tucked his hands against his chest, and turned his face to the floor.

Petra

PETRA WOKE TO an insistent tapping at his door, which continued unbroken as he struggled awake and out of his blankets. A hedgehog had burrowed against his hip sometime in the hours before dawn, and Petra folded the blankets back over her to keep her out of reach of the early-rising summer sun.

"Petra?" Sir Eckhart's voice reached him, muffled, through the door. "We need your help."

"Is it Fier?" Petra asked, then winced, unspeakably grateful that his voice came out as little more than a croak. This was a poor time to be groggy. "I'm awake!" he called, louder this time, and the knocking ceased.

"You only need to get dressed," Eckhart called, as Petra dragged on a clean shirt and apron. "This won't be gardening; bring no tools."

Petra unhooked his pendant from the nail over the door, brushed a spider from his canvas coat, pulled on both pendant and coat, and, doubling-back with an afterthought, pulled a new jar of honey from a shelf and stuck it in one of the oversized pockets.

Eckhart was waiting at the foot of the steps as Petra opened the door, her stance, as always, one of military formality. She looked as far from tired and disoriented as Petra felt, though she wore a small, pinched frown that tightened as Petra stumbled down the stairs.

"Here." She held out a bundle of linen, which Petra unfolded to find a triangular pastry, still warm and wreathed in the smell of almonds and cinnamon. "You may eat as we walk."

The knight led the way off the grounds and Petra, with one glance at the manor, followed at a trot. Though the sun had risen, the lingering morning chill crept beneath Petra's coat and left him shivering but far less sleepy.

Sir Eckhart offered no explanation (though she drew in a deep breath more than once, as if intending to), and with Petra trying to make as little a mess with the pastry as possible, they walked without speaking past the fountains and low sandstone walls of the town.

Eckhart had never woken him up for any sort of errand before. If he was not going to be asked to help with plants or to bring something out of the manor, Petra was at a loss as to what he might be needed for.

Maybe bats had blundered into someone's home again and were roosting out of reach, or maybe someone had found another moth the size of a closed fist and they hoped Petra would know what to do with it.

Their destination was not along the main streets: Eckhart strode through the central square without slowing and out to the rolling farmlands beyond. By then, Petra could hazard a guess as to which homestead they were headed.

Ten or twelve adults had gathered at the fence encircling the vegetable patch, although a few children stood on the wooden crossbars and jostled one another for a better view. Within the confines of the fence, a sheet of mist swirled over the ground. The sun, though not yet at full strength, should have burned it off, but the fog hung thick and pearlescent. As he and Sir Eckhart drew closer, Petra felt the temperature drop; the new cold burrowed into his chest and settled against his heart.

The onlookers turned at their approach, silent and expectant, and Eckhart led Petra up to the gate to the accompaniment of no sound save that of their footsteps in the grass. So many eyes on him made Petra's skin prickle with unease, but he did not, this time, feel the need to hide. They had asked for him; they had found, for once, a stranger presence than his.

He could see, through the twisting silver vapor,

the remains of the vegetable garden: leaves and stalks leeched of all color and weight, looking like nothing so much as thin, birdlike bones wedged at haphazard angles in the soil. None of them bore produce anymore, but a few ashen husks littered the ground beneath the leaves.

One of the onlookers cleared her throat. "The mist came in last night," she explained with forced unconcern, "but it was just a thin haze. Nothing like this."

"We've never seen *anything* like this," admitted another.

When Petra had first seen Fier's flower, it had felt unnatural – out of place. Bright and perfect, it made Petra's skin prickle, like something pulled out of the natural rhythms of the earth and folded into a separate world with its own set of rules. *This,* this clinging mist, felt more like... like those natural rhythms at full force. This, in its way, was magic, too: a thunderstorm before it broke, the stirring of a wildfire, a gathering of power beyond what humans could tame.

Watching the shifting sheet of mist, glimpsing again the bleached bones of the once-lustrous plant life, Petra's heart and stomach sank slowly into his toes.

He could make flowers grow. He could handle animals sick or dying or confused. That was all he could do. He could not handle *this*, whatever this was.

"I can't," he whispered. He glanced, apologetic, up at Sir Eckhart. "I don't think I can fix this."

If Eckhart was disappointed, she did not show it; she only nodded and touched a hand to his back, ready to steer him out of the crowd.

"Petra, please." Someone caught the edge of his jacket – the first of the onlookers. "We—"

"You heard him." Sir Eckhart turned a steely gaze on her. "He said no."

But the woman ignored Eckhart as if she had not heard the knight, had eyes for no one but Petra. "Please." Her voice, her expression, her bowed posture, was a plea. "We don't know who else to ask."

I just make the flowers grow, he wanted to say, to push this problem back onto her shoulders, but he bit his lip instead. They really did have no one else to ask – and they were afraid. He could see that now. How tightly they huddled together at the edge of the fence, the utter stillness as they waited for his answer. He should have seen as much from the start.

The manor left them – left all of them – with its paralyzing fear if they ventured too close; the fog carried no threat that he could feel, but it *was* strange, and strange was enough to lay the groundwork for panic. If he left now, the townsfolk would stand around the fence and fret and fret and fret. Maybe the mist and whatever caused it would go away – and maybe it wouldn't. Maybe it would spread. Maybe the absence of malice now was only temporary.

"I can't promise." His voice, though small, carried easily over those gathered. "But I can try."

Sir Eckhart's hand found his shoulder. "Are you sure?"

Petra nodded and turned back to the fence and the mist contained. Someone opened the gate. Petra touched the leather cord at his collar. He had remembered to tuck the pendant beneath his shirt, and he could feel the stone against his skin, its presence reassuring, if still cold. *Be good, be brave, be kind.*

With one final touch to his shoulder, Eckhart withdrew, and Petra stepped into the slowly-swirling mist.

A new wave of cold cut through Petra's coat, all the way through to his bones, and when he exhaled, his breath billowed up in a white cloud. His chest felt heavy, and he was uncomfortably aware of his heart pounding, but nothing else seemed to change. Whatever this fog was, it did not seem to be trying to keep him away; it did not seem aware of his presence at all.

A few steps deeper in, nothing changed. Nothing happened when the fog touched his skin. Nothing happened when he knelt to examine the fragile, bone-white stalks of the vegetable garden. Drained of life.

Drained of color. Why had this happened? If the mist had leeched the life out of the plants, would it do the same to people?

"Petra?" Eckhart's voice sounded muffled, as if from the other side of a closed door.

"I'm alright," Petra replied, then shut her and the other onlookers out of his thoughts. He closed his eyes and held very still. *Your feet are on the ground,* Nadeen had said. *You are here.* But the answer to this would not be found here, on the surface of the earth, wrapped in a mist he could not understand. So Petra pressed his bare hands against the cool, damp soil, tried to let go of the ground, of his heartbeat, of his mind. *Tell me what happened* asked without words, the answer listened for with the whole of his body.

The plants were dead. Their underground roots were shriveled and grey, as leeched of life as the stalks above. The carrots and radishes and turnips were nothing now but cavities in the earth, partially filled with the ashes of the once-growing.

But the fog was alive. Even with his eyes closed, Petra knew from a shift in the air around him that it curled around his head and shoulders. It was something alive – stagnant – stuck.

Something in nature's order *had* been thrown off. Bees swarmed every spring. Cocoons cracked into butterflies. Apples ripened and fell from their trees.

Life tumbled forward every day in a thousand little ways. So what, in this garden, was not moving? What had been stopped?

Tell me.

Bleached white bones buried in the soil. Petra could see them in his mind's eye, buried some short distance beneath him. He sank his hands into the freshly-tilled earth, and the soil offered as little resistance as water. Petra reached down, down, down, as deep as his elbows, and when his fingertips brushed something sharp and smooth, he grasped what he could and pulled it easily to the surface.

He held bones, mostly, with muscle and sinew enough to keep the skeleton in one stringy mass. As he cradled it to his chest, Petra opened his eyes, but inspected the clumps of fur and skin more with touch than with sight. This was not the body of a recently-killed animal, but the death, he knew, was days-old, no older than the mist.

This had been a rabbit. *Was* still a rabbit. This was what had become stuck. Listening to a voice almost too soft to hear, so faint that even his breathing was almost enough to drown it out, Petra struggled to stay out of his mind, out of his body. This was what had become stuck.

He needed to ask *why* and *what can be done*, but already he was on his feet and walking back to the fence, the rabbit dead and battered in his arms.

Those nearest the fence drew back as he approached – all except Eckhart, who watched him without blinking, her expression not one Petra was in a state of mind to decipher.

He held up the rabbit. "Who did this?"

No one answered, but Petra could wait. He could wait a long, long time.

Seconds passed, or minutes, or even an hour for all that Petra could keep track. Eventually a soft "I did," broke the silence and a child stepped forward from the front ranks of those gathered. No older than ten or twelve, his hair was an untrimmed golden mess, his skin tawny. He hid his hands behind his back, but Petra had a chance to see they were shaking.

"You did this."

The boy hunched his shoulders and ducked his chin into his scarf in a manner more defensive than apologetic. "I just… It was with a sling. I wanted to see if I could hit it."

"You killed her for sport."

"I didn't mean to."

An untimely and purposeless death. Was that enough to throw the balance? Human cruelty was nothing new. Death of the hunted was nothing new. Why this bottled power here? Why this bottled power now?

With his mind stretching thin thin thin, Petra felt the answer slide out of reach. Some part of him kept insisting the boy was a lion cub, with the scruffy beginnings of a mane and paws to grow into. Staying twice-awake might have been easier if he had still been half-asleep, but there was nothing for it now but to dig in his heels and keep his eyes open.

"She needs a different burial. Come here."

The boy hesitated. One of the adults behind jolted forward a step. Eckhart glanced in their direction, touched the hilt of the sword at her hip.

"It must be you." Petra drifted closer, just one step, and proffered what remained of the rabbit. "I will help."

Another waiting, this one shorter than the first. The straight line of the boy's mouth became thinner and thinner as he stared at the body, until finally the stillness broke with a sharp and sudden nod, and his hands came up to take the rabbit from Petra.

Instinct drew Petra back into the garden, to the foot of the only living plant remaining within the boundaries of the fence: a low-branched beech tree. He crouched at the roots and the boy, trailing through the mist behind him, did the same.

"Wrap her in something of yours."

With one hand, the boy tugged the faded orange scarf from around his neck and tried to bundle the rabbit into it. His hands were still shaking. Petra placed one hand under the bulk of the rabbit to hold it steady and helped to loop the scarf with the other.

"You have nothing to fear."

"I'm not afraid," the boy retorted. The hitch in his voice betrayed him.

"Now," Petra continued, easing the now-bundled body out of the boy's hands, "dig."

While Petra had been able to reach into the earth as if the soil was not there at all, the boy had no such ease. He scooped out small, hard-won handfuls of dirt, his fingernails soon caked black with the effort. Petra did not help this time, but sat with his teeth gritted and a headache gathering behind his temples. He had to remind himself to breathe, and his heart was a slow, leaden stammer in his chest. A bone had broken off from the skeleton's spinal cord, and even though it was thin and angular and alien against his palm, Petra did not drop it. It would be needed.

When the new grave was deep enough for the boy's arms to be dirtied up to the elbows, Petra pushed past the pain in his head and his chest to listen again. Listening *hurt* – like sinking his fingers into ice water. *What next* he asked, and he heard himself answer: "Sing."

"Sing?" The boy blinked up at him. "Sing what?"

"Anything."

The boy cleared his throat, but made no other sound. Andrei – that was his name. As Petra lay the rabbit at the bottom of the grave and began to push the earth back into place, Andrei began to sing. His voice was thin with nerves, but clear, and Petra recognized the words as part of a nursery rhyme – a lullaby to help children fall asleep:

"Rest your weary head, my dear,
And close your eyes upon the night.
When you wake, I shall be here,
Even if I'm not in sight."

The lullaby had three verses, but at the end of the first, Andrei began it again, and Petra sang with him. Again and again, the same verse, over and over and over, Andrei's voice stronger with each repetition and Petra's wavering as the cold in his chest spread past his ribs.

By the time Andrei smoothed the last of the earth over the rabbit's resting place, Petra almost couldn't see for the pounding in his head. He could feel his pulse in his wrists, in his throat, against the back of his teeth.

"You have nothing to fear," he said again, the words wrenched out of him. He had one of Andrei's hands in his own. He pressed the salvaged bone into the boy's palm. "Wear this on a string. Wear it around your neck. Wear it until the string wears through."

Andrei nodded. Tears had left tracks down his cheeks, and there was a smudge of dirt against his nose where he had tried to wipe them away.

"This be done. And the world turns."

At once, the frigid weight vanished from Petra's chest, and he gasped, his breathing unencumbered at last, his body his own, his mind his own.

The fog, a shining silver, swirled around the pair of them crouched over the new grave. Petra caught a glimpse of what must have been the entire town ranged along the edge of the fence before the mist spun faster, gleaming in the sun, and blocked the on-lookers from view. For a moment – just a moment, so brief Petra almost missed it with a blink – the twisting silver resolved into a doe – a long-legged, long-necked doe taller at the shoulder than Petra – with a silver rabbit twining through her legs.

Then the mist was gone altogether, as if it had never been, and the vegetable garden beside them was as green and verdant as it had been before, and the only proof of the whole ordeal was the bone still cupped in Andrei's palm.

The cold might have been gone, but the head-ache remained, and it was almost all Petra could do just to stagger to his feet. Andrei bolted for the gate;

Petra limped after. He could still feel his pulse all down his arms, and his heartbeat kicked so strongly now that he pressed a hand against his chest to keep his heart from beating out of his body.

As he neared the gate, a wave of dizziness left everyone's faces blurred, but Petra had a glimpse of two women side-by-side in one of the front rows – the women from the raspberry picking. He'd almost forgotten.

He could hear Eckhart speaking, could hear her striding across the grass in his direction, but Petra ignored her, staggered over to the pair of women instead, fumbled in his pocket for the nearly-forgotten jar of honey.

"This is for you." He pushed it into their hands. He couldn't hear his voice, but surely he was speaking. "Thank you for the coat."

Eckhart caught up with him, then, just as his legs gave out, and Petra sank into the knight's arms with a sigh that seemed to purge all the air from his body and fainted.

- - -

Petra woke to birdsong and muted sunlight, and he opened his eyes unto an unfamiliar ceiling. The high wooden beams of the gatekeeper's cottage had bundles of herbs and tiny glass jars held aloft with string. These had been left bare.

He gazed at the new, naked ceiling for a while, too tired to properly wonder where he was. He lay on a bed, covered by a quilt and, over that, his barn coat had been spread like a blanket over his chest. His hands, when he held them up for inspection, were free from dirt, though his shirtsleeves still bore the shadows of a morning spent digging. Hopefully whoever had put him here had remembered to remove his boots.

The headache was gone, and the chill had left his chest. Tucked beneath the quilt as he was, with the sun streaming in through a window on his right, Petra could not quite believe that the freezing weight in his chest had been anything but a dream.

But, he realized, glancing at the open window, this was Eckhart's home: Only Eckhart kept such golden flowers on each of her windowsills. If this was Eckhart's home, then Petra really had collapsed in the garden, which meant that the morning's burial had been real and not a dream.

Almost as a reflex, Petra touched his collar, ran his thumb and forefinger along the leather cord he knew would be there, would always be there. Had he been in danger? The mist – the doe – had not felt malicious, and she had wanted only reparation, but a blizzard or a flood could cause harm without meaning to. How close to death had Petra come in trying to speak with her?

What would have happened if he had died? The gatekeeper's cottage was not his, of course, nor was anything in it. The townsfolk could recollect their long-lent gifts, and everything else, every growing thing left in pot and jar and barrel, would spill out into the gardens given time.

No one would know where to find Iris, if they had a mind to tell her.

No one would tell Fier.

Petra's heart constricted at that. Fier would wait, day after day, for Petra to come, and Petra never would, and no one would be able to tell Fier what had happened. Fier would never know that Petra hadn't meant to leave. Maybe the prince would assume that Petra had simply tired of seeing him. Maybe he would fall and stay asleep until the next time someone accidentally woke him up, and even then, he might never know what had stolen Petra away.

Petra would miss him. Or perhaps not. Was death such that you could grieve for what you had left behind? If so, then yes, Petra would miss him – miss him dearly. He would miss so much: the sun against his skin, the background hum of bees and cicadas, the taste of water when he'd gone too long without a drink. He would miss picking fruit in the summer and finding the first green hints of spring in the last of the melting snow. He would miss waking on winter mornings to find foxes curled under the blankets with him for warmth and company. He would even miss sitting awkwardly next to Eckhart during the fall festivals, delightfully full but uneasy with so many laughing, tipsy near-strangers on all sides.

And Fier. As much as all the rest together.

The tread of booted feet tugged Petra's attention to the room's only doorway just as Sir Eckhart stepped through, a book tucked under her arm and a wooden mug cupped in her hands.

"You're awake." Her voice was low and calm, even soothing. "How are you feeling?"

"Fine, I think."

The knight set book and mug on the otherwise-empty bedside table and helped Petra sit up. Petra made no protest as she drew him upright and wedged pillows behind his shoulders. She rearranged his coat over his lap with more care than may have been strictly necessary, then handed him the mug. The contents must have been tea: Petra could smell mint in its thin curl of steam.

As Petra took a tentative sip, careful not to burn his tongue, Eckhart retrieved an oak chair from the other side of the nightstand and dropped into it. She leaned forward at once, her elbows propped on her knees, and fixed Petra with her penetrating gaze.

"You do feel alright?"

"Yes. How long did I sleep?"

"Nearly the whole day. Dusk is a few hours off."

Then he still had time to visit Fier. Petra took another sip of tea, not sure what to say. Eckhart seemed in no hurry to speak, either, so Petra, not sure what else would suit, settled at last on, "I'm sorry I worried you."

"You worried everyone."

"Oh." Petra set the mug of tea in his lap. He should have expected as much. He had spoken to ghosts; he had forced a child to handle the skin and bones of a dead creature. If the townsfolk had been afraid of him before, they would be terrified now. They already thought him a witch. What would be worse than that?

"Do you know what you did this morning?"

"I didn't do anything. I just listened. That's all."

"Petra."

"That's all I did."

"*Petra*," Eckhart insisted, and Petra curled his fingers more tightly around the mug, braced himself for her fear, too, her fear at last. "I know witchcraft is something they have trained you to see as dangerous. I know that hurts you."

Petra didn't look up from his mug of tea. He could see shreds of leaf floating at the bottom. He could smell honey, too. Honey and mint.

"But you are not a danger, Petra." Eckhart rested a hand against his wrist; Petra did not pull away. "Plants that have no business in this climate thrive around you. You plant dead roots and a garden blooms. You spoke for the dead today. You *are* a witch, Petra, of the best kind. You calm, you heal, you strengthen that which grows."

He could not take another sip of tea without betraying the shaking in his hands, and neither could he look at Eckhart. She had never spoken to him so freely before, and Petra did not know if he deserved her softened edges.

Beside him, the knight withdrew her hand and leaned back in the chair. "You gave a jar of honey to Alma and Cora this morning. Why?"

Oh, so those were their names. "They gave me this coat." Petra lifted his hands enough to properly reveal the barn-coat-turned-blanket. "I wanted to give them something, too."

"They told me, the other day, that you had been very sweet with Maria. They said they'd never seen you smile before. And Maria has since lost her raspberry beetle, but she has yet to stop telling everyone how you found it for her."

Petra risked looking up. Sir Eckhart, like Fier, did not (and had never) seem bothered by the tarnish of his face. Her mouth, so often severe, was tilted in a smile.

"You do seem... different." Her voice, too, was gentle. "More awake."

"I've been unconscious."

"Beyond that. You've always been shy, but when Nadeen passed away and Iris left, you fell into yourself. You were almost a ghost of your own."

Iris. Homesickness swooped through his stomach, so strong a surge it left him ill, and Petra dropped his gaze again to his lap.

Sometimes at night, if he lay on his back and closed his eyes, he could almost feel Nadeen at one shoulder, Iris at the other, both of them close and solid and warm against him. The rhythm of their breath in sleep was the most soothing sound he could remember.

Most often, Nadeen would lay with his back to them, and Petra would lean against him in the dark, facing Iris, who would push her forehead against his and talk, talk, talk in hushed tones. The two of them could stay like that for hours before falling asleep, tucked in a private world beneath the blankets, whispering secrets that, years later, seemed small and silly: Iris's quiet, proud confessions to kissing one of the cook's daughters; Petra's barely-audible concerns that he was responsible for all the spiders in the tool shed; their oft-voiced dreams of working as a pair forever, Iris as the merchant and Petra as the gardener, never the one without the other.

"I miss her," he admitted, in a voice so small he did not expect Eckhart to hear him.

But hear him she did. "She was your best friend. You will always miss her."

"She promised to write."

"She still could."

"I still wish she'd come back."

Eckhart gave no reply, and Petra took another sip of tea as if doing so did not threaten to dislodge the lump in his throat. Iris was not coming back. He knew that. He had known that from the day she left.

"It's a painful gift," Eckhart said softly, "loving someone with a restless heart. They take part of you with them when they go. And Iris took a great piece of you when she left."

Petra could not argue. Everyone had known, had seldom seen the one without the other. Wherever Iris went, Petra trailed after, as constant as if tethered.

"But there's more of you here than there was before. Something has been drawing you out." Eckhart studied him, then as always: as if she could see right through to his heart. "You seem to be waking up," she went on. "I wonder why."

Petra knew why. Green eyes bright with unconcealed affection. An unbound smile and a flurry of greetings – *How are you how did you sleep I missed you.*

Rainy mornings sequestered in their bubble of calm. Hours upon hours of sunlight and idleness. *You're beautiful, you know.* A precious flower in a cloudy glass jar.

"He's alive."

Sir Eckhart closed her eyes, and Petra could see her exhale, could see the tension recede from her shoulders as she let go, in one long breath, of three years of mingled hope and fear. She'd known – or hoped or suspected – and Petra could feel her relief as strongly as if it were his own: wires uncoiling from around his heart, melting to nothing in the wash of heat through his chest and stomach.

"I'm sorry. I should have told you sooner."

"Don't be sorry. How is he?"

"He's kind." He paused when Eckhart nodded, as if she'd known as much. "Bright. Like a star."

"Good." Eckhart's mouth wavered into a trembling smile. "Very good."

"So bright he's blinding."

"Full of questions?"

"So many." Petra fought a smile of his own, failed, and hid it behind the uplifted mug of tea. "And all in earnest."

"Is he happy?"

Petra's stomach twisted. Fier seemed delighted with so little: just the sun or music or someone to sit with. What anyone else might have taken for granted,

Fier took as the greatest gifts in the world. But for all his radiance when he was happy, Fier was so often, so easily, so far from happiness.

"Sir," he began, "he's still cursed. He's hurt. He's afraid, and I don't know what he's afraid of."

Eckhart, too, resettled into seriousness, though her pose remained loose. "Just listen to him." A frisson of pain crossed her features, there then gone. "Be patient and listen. You are the only one who can go into the manor, Petra. If Fier is suffering – is still suffering – then I think you might be the one to help him recover."

"Because I'm a witch."

"Because, Petra, you're the best of us." Eckhart leaned forward, her eyes dark and shining and intense. "You help everyone you can, however you can. You help out of love, a quiet and steady love, and that's a powerful gift when freely given. You're *full* of love. You can't fight Fier's anguish for him, but you can help him see a way through to the other side."

Petra knew his face was burning, and his heart was lodged uncomfortably in his throat, but this was not childhood teasing or flippancy. This was what he knew already: be good, be brave, be kind. "Yes, sir."

"No matter what happens, I am proud of you." Eckhart stood and rested a hand heavy on his shoulder. "You *do* feel alright?"

"I think so."

"Good. But you've eaten nothing all day, and I'm not sending you home until you do."

Petra

BY THE TIME Eckhart had ensured he was properly fed and watered, the sun had set and the last of the orange and pink on the horizon had faded to the dark, uniform blue of night. Petra stepped out into the night with a borrowed lantern and a final wave of farewell.

The streets around him were deserted, as they often were after dark, but candles glowed on windowsills, nearby and in the distance, and lit the sleeping town with scattered constellations of light. As he padded along the clean-swept brick paths, Petra could hear voices low in conversation, a loud laugh with a "Shh!" on its heels, snatches of singing.

Bats swooped in handfuls in the darkness over the town, shadow upon shadow. One landed on the back of his shoulder with a soft *thump*. It crept up the back of his coat, pressed its nose against his neck in quick inspection, and departed with a flap of leathery wings.

Early mornings were his favorite time of day,

but there was a charm to evenings, too. Everything became slower, quieter, softer. Walking alone at night had its own kind of solitude, as if other people existed only in the margins, each wrapped up in their private, faraway worlds. People at night were like stars: bright but distant, self-contained.

Alone, truly alone, for the first time all day, Petra basked in the solitude. The night was full of music: crickets and cicadas in every green corner, familiar and half-heard lullabies drifting from open windows, the trickle of narrow streams winding undisturbed through town. Fireflies wafted up from the banks of the streams, drifted like sparks on the breeze, blinking on and off, on and off to a rhythm no one else could hear.

And while all around him was peaceful and beautiful, Petra's thoughts turned toward Fier. The prince exiled himself from so much, and Petra felt a stab of grief for the tragedy of it, for whatever had scarred him so deeply that *this* – the wide and wonderful world with its sun and stars and thousand tiny treasures – seemed worth sacrificing.

He had never visited Fier after dark before, but he owed the prince an apology for leaving him unexpectedly alone from dawn until dusk. Did Fier sleep? He was always awake when Petra found him in the morning, even before the prince's flower had been set upright and watered.

Petra delayed only long enough to fill a flask from one of the garden's ponds, then to dislodge a frog that squatted on his hand and refused to be tipped in among the lilies. Eventually, with the flask in the pocket of his apron and the borrowed lantern cradled in both hands, he turned his steps at last to the manor. Fireflies rising up out of the grass at his feet, each one a small, glowing sun.

The house was dark at night, darker than he had expected. Even on rainy days, the walls and furniture had been some shade of grey, but at night, every doorway was an open mouth, the depths of the rooms beyond impenetrable. Petra's lantern cast a ring of golden light a few scant feet in every direction, and every time he moved, shifting black shadows caught the corners of his eyes. The silence, usually echoing, felt oppressive, as heavy as a funeral cloth, and Petra winced at the sound of his steps on the wooden floor.

Fier's door was mostly closed when he reached it, though Petra had left it wide open at his last visit. This house was old enough that its balance must have shifted, either in the hinges of the door or in the foundation of the house itself.

"Fier?" he called softly, in case the prince was indeed asleep. He touched the edge of the door with two fingers, pushed it open on silent hinges. "Fier, are you--"

It loomed as dark as a void, crouched on legs half-formed, its arms hanging handless and melting in strings, its head and shoulders hunched over the flower on the rug – and wrenched itself out of sight so quickly Petra might have doubted he'd seen it at all had he not felt it whip past him in a blur of cold so intense it left him shaking. It was gone – and the flower was still there – and Fier sat curled in the corner, his knees drawn to his chest, his eyes shut, his face tight with grim resolve, his hands twisted viciously into his hair.

Petra dropped the lantern and was on his knees beside him in a heartbeat. "Fier – are you hurt? Did it hurt you?"

The prince's eyes flew open, but they were glassy and flat and without recognition. Petra realized with a start that he was shaking – Fier was shaking – and panting – out of breath with his blinding panic.

"Fier – it's okay – it's gone. It's okay. It's okay."

He reached out to touch, to soothe, forgetting that was impossible, but the prince jerked away from Petra's hand and recoiled deeper into his corner. "Don't *touch* me!" he hissed, pushing at – through – Petra's arm.

Petra withdrew at once, and was halfway to his feet to retreat farther when Fier's eyes snapped back into focus. "Wait – Wait!" he gasped, still curled away, his arms still held up like a shield. "Don't leave, please don't leave."

"I won't leave." Petra dropped back onto his knees, tucked his arms inside his coat where they would not be a threat to Fier. "I'm right here."

"I'm sorry. I'm sorry." Fier dropped one knee, made a feeble attempt to uncurl himself. His hands were buried in his hair again, and his eyes were screwed shut against the tears that gathered in his eyelashes. "I didn't want this to happen with you."

"It's okay. It's okay. You don't have to be sorry."

Fier rocked forward until his forehead was pressed against the bedroom floor, every line of him tight with ill-concealed, ill-controlled panic. "I didn't want this to happen with you," he said again, his voice hitching, and Petra thought his heart would break.

"You haven't done anything wrong," he promised, but words seemed useless against so much pain, and Petra scrambled in the dark for some way to soothe him. Touch was easiest – was what felt most natural – but he would not have tried that now even if he could.

Fier remained motionless on the floor, except for the tremors in his shoulders, and Petra could hear his breath catching as he tried so desperately to keep from crying. Petra had calmed him, that first day, with that rambling talk of flowers, but his mind was a blank slate, empty of everything except Fier hurt, Fier afraid, Fier crying. He opened his mouth, closed it, tried on a whim to hum their piano music, could not remember the tune of it, and gave his voice to the only song he *could* remember:

"Rest your weary head, my dear,
And close your eyes upon the night.
When you wake, I shall be here,
Even if I'm not in sight."

He could not recall ever singing by himself before, and while his voice echoed strangely in the dark, empty room, he could hear, too, Fier's sudden, shaky silence. Andrei had wanted only the first verse, but Petra drifted easily into the second and third.

"The dawn, she comes on silent wings,
As she has done for years gone by.
The dark, there's nothing it can bring
To dim the fire in your eyes.

"So rest your weary head, my dear,
And fear not what you see in sleep.
Wherever you go, you'll have me near.
You have my love and heart to keep."

Fier made no sound at all. He might have been holding his breath, and he had tilted his head as if to better catch the words. Far too relieved to feel self-conscious, Petra began again, sang the whole again, was ready to sing until his voice gave out if that would help.

The last words of the reprisal echoed briefly, then faded, and silence settled. Fier had stopped crying, if the stillness of his shoulders was anything to go by, but he did not raise his head. But he seemed to be out of his panic; the only thing now was to give him time and space enough to recover.

"I'm not going anywhere," Petra promised again as he rose slowly to his feet. He retrieved the lantern, found the glass jar in the darkness under the bed, re-filled it with the water from his flask, and set the flower inside. He brought this back to a still-unmoving Fier and set it within the scope of the lantern's glow.

Before he sat down, he shut the bedroom door, debated locking it, refrained, and sat against the wall beside his friend, able now to keep an eye on the door as if vigilance alone might ward away the manor's other occupant.

Eventually, Fier sat up with a cough to clear his throat and pushed his hair back from his face. "I've never heard that song before," he whispered. His cheeks and nose shone with the tracks of his tears, but he had indeed stopped crying. "What was it?"

"A lullaby." Petra held still, very still, as Fier settled against the wall beside him. He kept his hands tucked into his coat, just in case. "Are you okay?"

"Not yet." Fier rocked his head back against the wall – or nearly so. "It will pass."

"What was that thing?"

"The beast, I guess." Talking must have brought him some sort of relief, or maybe continued silence was unpalatable, but either way, once begun, Fier didn't seem able to stop: "It doesn't hurt me, and it never sees me, or if it does, it doesn't care. I think it only comes in here for the flower, but it never does anything except knock it over – or that's all I can see, anyway. When it gets too close to... to it, the nightmares start, and when I wake up, it's gone."

"It's come here before?"

"Yes, every night."

"*Every* night?"

"Yes." Fier pushed back his hair again. "I didn't tell you. I didn't want you to know. I didn't... want you to know."

Every night. Petra felt sick and unsteady. His tucked-in hands were as much a precaution against startling Fier as they were to keep himself from shaking.

Fier had been attacked every night, every night from the very beginning, and Petra had never even known it was happening. He had never even thought to ask.

"It's never getting near you again." Petra's voice was wound tight with urgency and what he recognized distantly as anger. "It's not going to hurt you again. I won't let it."

"You can't," Fier protested. "It might hurt *you*."

"It won't. I don't care if it does."

"I can manage. It could be worse."

"Fier, you're *suffering*. It's *attacking* you. You don't have to go through this *every night*."

"Yes, I do. If that's the cost of staying as I am, then I'll pay it." Fier was trembling again, his hands clasped in his lap, his gaze bright and fierce and focused. "I'll pay it," he said again, "and you can't get rid of it. It's mine to fight."

Every time Petra closed his eyes, he could see the shadow-creature's melting arms, the sticky strings of it curling around the fallen flower. *You can't fight his anguish for him.*

"I won't get rid of it," he promised. "I wouldn't know how, anyway. But neither am I going to leave you to face that thing by yourself."

"What if you scaring it away was a fluke? What if it comes back? What if it *kills* you?"

"It won't come back. It can't." Petra reached past

the neck of his shirt, closed his hand over the stone at his heart, and looped the cord up and over his head. "We can use this," he explained, presenting with an open hand the pendant to Fier.

Fier froze, and his surprise was so obvious that it flooded Petra, too, whipping through his stomach and stirring up the beat of his heart. He had expected puzzlement, not recognition, and he drew back the stone at once, cupped it in both hands to hide it from sight.

"Where did you get that?"

"I've had it for years."

"That's what she tried to give me." Fier blinked, came back to himself. His eyes nearly glowed as he looked up from the shield of Petra's hands. "That night, when she came to the door, that's what the witch tried to give me."

Fier

PETRA, TO HIS CREDIT, looked more confused than distrustful. "I've had this since I was twelve – three years before you moved here."

But Fier would have recognized that stone anywhere. He saw it often enough in the tumult of dream and memory before he woke each morning. Small enough and smooth enough to be a river pebble, that nearly-perfect hole bored through the center. Held by a grey, wrinkled, claw-like hand. The talons of a vulture.

"Who gave it to you?"

"A woman." Petra had yet to stop watching him, his eyes dark and worried, but at Fier's barest nod, he continued: "She came to the cottage while Nadeen and Iris were away on a two-day errand. At nearly midnight, in the middle of a storm, she knocked on the door."

"You were alone? And you answered?"

"I couldn't leave someone in the rain and the cold. She had blood on her hands. She asked for a rag. She said she'd fallen."

Fier did not remember the witch being injured, but the image of a hunched figure in rain-soaked grey, hooded against the tearing wind and rain sprang easily to mind. "Was she old?"

"Not elderly, no. More like a mother."

"With blood on her hands."

Petra shrugged. "I gave her the rag. I tried to give her bread and fruit, and I tried to get her to come in, so she could spend the night somewhere warm and dry, but she just smiled and refused everything but the rag. She pressed the stone into my hand and said, 'A token for your kindness, little one. Wear this and be safe.' Then she left."

A token, Your Grace. In exchange for something warm to eat.

Petra had opened his door to a woman strange and bloodied; he had been alone and young and still he had tried to give her so much more than she had asked for. He was generous and kind and trusting and *good*, and Fier had faced nothing but an old woman, and he'd been too wound up and sick with fear to even think of helping her.

"Fier? Was that your witch, too?"

"No." Fier wished, for the first time in years, for

a cloak or a blanket to draw up over his head, something to hide beneath and stay under forever. "Mine was an old woman, and she wasn't covered in blood. She wanted something to eat. I didn't give her anything. But you – you gave yours so much – and you were alone."

"You can't compare the two."

Of course – *of course* – Petra would say that. Fier pulled up his knees and wrapped his arms around them. Petra's eyes were on him still, and Fier pushed his face against his knees, hid as best he could. He couldn't see him. He didn't want to see him.

"Fier, I did the best I could, and you did the best you could. You *can't* compare the two."

"Stop." Fier knew his voice was a fractured mess and he didn't care. He didn't care. His face was burning; his eyes were burning; his chest was burning. "I was heartless. I didn't care – I just wanted her to go. I didn't care. I was heartless."

"Fier. Don't say that."

"I was. I was, I was, I was."

"That's not--"

"I tried to hit her. She grabbed my arm and-- and I hurt Eckhart, too. I *hit* her and I *never* told her I was sorry."

He didn't look up to see how Petra took that, but he didn't need to. He shut his eyes at a new wave of regret so strong it left him shaking. He could feel Sir Eckhart's touch on his wrist, could hear *We can find somewhere else for you to sleep* in a tone meant to soothe. He could see, all too easily, the shock, the sorrow, the hurt that took over the whole of her face.

"Fier, listen to me." Petra's voice was a blanket, a balm, and Fier shook his head, but Petra kept going: "Fier. You're not heartless. Your heart is right there. I pick it up every day, and it's the most beautiful thing I've ever seen. You're not heartless. And Eckhart knows that, too. She still loves you. She is *always* going to love you. And *I* love you--"

Whatever else Petra might have said, Fier did not hear it. Blood rushed into his ears and obliterated every sound but the ceaseless hammering of his own heart.

Eckhart loved him. Despite his constant, fractious conduct, despite his absolute and utter failure to grow into the prince she fought so hard for him to be, Eckhart loved him. And Petra – *Petra* – loved him. Petra saw him in sharp, jagged pieces and loved him. Petra stayed with him through the slow hours of lazy summer days when they had nothing to do and loved him. Petra *loved him*, and every bottled hope shattered open at once and flooded Fier with an unbound joy so sudden and so strong it left him dizzy.

Petra loves everyone. Fier knew that, and forced

himself calm. Petra helped everyone, cared for everyone, chose to love everyone. Anyone who walked into a cursed manor to retrieve a hat or tried to usher a blood-soaked possible-murderess of the rain was *absolutely* full of love. Petra acted out of kindness and generosity and love, and Fier swept up the shattered glass and tried to bury the contents. Petra loved everyone, gave so easily the gift of his heart, and Petra would not want Fier's in return.

"Fier?"

Against his will, Fier looked up, and found Petra trying to catch his eye, his mouth a small and worried frown until Fier reluctantly met his gaze. And then, for what must have been the first time in their friendship, Petra smiled, smiled at *him*, with that painfully soft, adoring smile Fier had only ever seen bestowed upon the gardens, and if Fier had not been melted already, he would have melted then.

"You have a good heart, Fier, and I will tell you that every day until you believe me."

"I'm sorry. Tell her I'm sorry."

The smile faded from Petra's mouth but not his eyes. "I will."

"And I want to tell you how... how everything happened."

That sobered the gardener. "Are you sure?"

"Yes." He was terrified still – and might be always

– of dismissal, of disbelief, but he could try one more time. Just one more time. "I'm sure."

"Okay."

"I'll have to explain a… a lot of things."

"Anything you need. I'll listen."

"Okay. But I can't-- I can't look at you while I'm talking about it. Or I don't-- I guess I don't want you to look at me. That's too much."

"Do you want me to close my eyes?"

"No, I… I think I have a better idea."

- - -

Within a few minutes, they had their arrangement. Petra lay on the rug, settled on top of the heap of blankets Fier had insisted he drag off the bed. He had removed his boots and apron to leave by the closed door, and he had bundled his coat beneath his head as a pillow. Fier lay beside him, an arm-span away. The flower in its jar stood between them; Petra had looped the leather cord around it several times, and the witch's stone pendant sat propped against the base of the glass.

"You can't fall asleep until I'm done."

"I won't. I promise."

"Okay." Fier fixed his gaze on a crack in the ceiling. "I'm going to start."

"I'm listening."

He drew in a deep breath and let it out slowly.

"When I was a kid, I had dance lessons with some of the other children in the palace. Our instructor wanted to teach us the waltz, but at that age, we mostly wanted to chase each other around the ballroom.

"But I *loved* dancing. I loved being so close to another person, and I loved how we had to learn to move together like two halves of the same body.

"The girl I usually partnered with was named Rosa, and we were close outside of dance lessons, too. We held hands when we played together, which was often, and she always gave me a hug when we met before dinner or after dinner or at any chance meeting between.

"I *loved* touching. I would have been that close to everyone all the time, but my family didn't... didn't really want me to be that affectionate with them, and I could tell hugs made Sir Eckhart uncomfortable, so Rosa was really all I had, but that was okay. She was wonderful. For years, she was wonderful.

"And then... we grew up." Fier could feel his stomach sinking again, as if this, the whole mess of it, had happened yesterday and not so many years ago. "Everything was fine until we were about fourteen or fifteen, and then... then dancing wasn't what it had been. Nothing was. Instead of leaving her hand on my shoulder, Rosa would... would creep her fingers up onto my neck. When we weren't dancing, she would come up behind me and lean against my back. If we were sitting next to each other for dinner, she would put her hand on my knee.

"I started to feel like every time she touched me, she wanted something else, but I couldn't understand what that was. I couldn't understand why what we'd had wasn't enough anymore. But we had been friends for so long, and we had always been so close, I didn't know how to ask her to stop. I tried, but I don't think I tried hard enough. She didn't seemed to hear me."

Beside him, Petra made a low, possibly involuntary sound of sympathy, but Fier paused only long enough to take another breath before he plunged onward.

"If anyone noticed what she was doing, they never said so. The only person I ever mentioned anything to was Eckhart, and she said Rosa was just showing that she liked me. Since I liked her, too, and I wanted to be close, I... I... I went along with it. With everything. Even though the mystery of it made me feel sick.

"And then, one night after dinner, when we were alone in the hallway, she grabbed me and dragged me into an empty room and slid her hand up my shirt." There was another, sharper sound of protest from Petra, but Fier ignored it, grateful that Petra couldn't see him. Fier could monitor his expression or make sure his voice was as flat and matter-of-fact as possible, but not both. Not now.

I thought you liked me.

I do! Of course I do!

If you did, you would do this with me.

"All the times I wanted her to stop and all those times I wanted to push her away, they all came crashing back at once, and I-- I panicked. I don't remember much of it. I know I shouted at her. I just kept shouting. I don't know what I said, and probably I shoved her – much too hard. I never saw her after that. I think her parents took her away.

"I thought that would be the end of it, but I was wrong. What she wanted – what she wanted *from me* – was what other people wanted, too. I kept thinking 'This time will be different,' and I kept making friends with all of the young women introduced to me by my family. I was supposed to pick one of them to marry, and if marriage had meant holding hands and hugs instead of kisses or… or anything else, I would have married in a heartbeat.

"But all of them had grown up in a way I hadn't. All of them wanted something I didn't. The young men, too: when I talked with them, the conversation almost always veered toward the… the bedroom and which of our peers they would take into it, and I didn't want that, any of it.

"And all the time, whenever I had to dance at parties, I couldn't forget what Rosa's hand felt like creeping up my neck. Sometimes I can still feel it. And whenever my partners' hands wandered from where they were supposed to be, I would get so... so *sick*. And their hands wandered so often. I would ask them not to touch me like that, but they did anyway. Rosa happened over and over and over again. I panicked. I always panicked. I would yell and shove and get away. Every time.

"No one believed me when I said I didn't want to be touched like that. 'You'll change your mind eventually, Fier,' and 'You don't have to lie to *us*, Fier,' and 'Don't be so stubborn, Fier.' And it was so bad. It was *so bad*."

The memories were snapping at his thoughts like a pack of wild dogs. The press of fingers against his wrist – at first a welcome touch, then a dangerous one. Someone whispering in his ear as they passed him in the ballroom, their breath hot and damp and horrible against his neck. An arm slung around his waist like a vice. Crude jokes, an impossible subtext, the gentle caress of hands and face cheapened to fodder for an endless, pervasive hunger for *more than this*.

"It was so bad." Fier pressed the heels of his hands against his eyes. No tears. He could feel them gathering in his chest, ready to crash into him in a great and terrible wave, but no tears. Not now. *All of that is over*, he insisted. *None of that is ever going to happen to you again. This is better. This is so much better.*

"On the... the night of the curse, the woman I was dancing with put her hand on my neck and, of course, I panicked. I don't remember what I said or did. I don't remember anything except wanting to get away. And then Sir Eckhart got in the way and caught my wrist and that's why I... I hit her. I wasn't thinking. And before I could apologize, there was a knock on the door, and there was the witch, and... and here we are."

For a long, long time, Petra said nothing, and Fier lay with his hands over his eyes, struggling to breathe as slowly and quietly as he could. Petra was not looking at him – he had promised not to look – but still Fier felt far too exposed, far too precarious to be balanced on the hair-thin line between hope and resignation. The waiting was the worst part.

"Fier. What's your favorite flower?"

Of all the responses he had expected, that was not one of them, and Fier raised his hands from his eyes, shot a glance at Petra's silhouette. As promised, Petra was not looking at him and spoke instead to the ceiling.

When Fier said nothing, Petra continued, his voice just as soft as before. "I think people pick their favorite flowers for how they look or how they smell or how easy they are to take care of. Some people only want to look at them, some people want to plant them, and some people want to trim them and take them home. People love differently, for different reasons and in different ways. You don't have to want flowers in the same way other people want them. There's nothing wrong with you, Fier. You know that, don't you? There's nothing wrong with you."

For fourteen years, Fier had closed his eyes in the hours before sleep and imagined scene after scene of what he knew he would never have. When he was seven, he had imagined being swept off his feet by an explorer or a wandering knight or a pirate – someone who wouldn't care about succession or cold parents or kings and queens.

By fifteen, he had realized that he did not, actually, want to live as a pirate, and so he had dreamed instead of whispered confessions in the ballroom and joined hands and shared, secretive smiles.

By eighteen, when he and Eckhart had relocated to the manor, when all he had dared to really hope for had been, "Once for a child, and then never again," he had found refuge in imagining a lover who would catch him up in a bearlike hug and promise instead, "This is enough. This is more than enough, and I love you for you, and I want you happy." He had imagined, in every iteration, ricocheting joy and tears and a relief so strong he could not breathe.

He had not once imagined understanding given so casually, with so little fanfare, as he lay still shaking with nausea and a slowly-receding panic in the lantern-lit darkness of his bedroom.

"Fier? You know that, don't you? There's nothing wrong with you."

"Sunflowers." A face caught in sunlight, outlined in gold. A small, private smile turned up to the unclouded sky. "Sunflowers are my favorite."

Petra didn't say anything to that, but Fier wouldn't have known what to do if he had. He'd never seen this side of the conversation before. *You won't feel that way forever* and *I can change your mind* and the resultant heave of betrayal were all he had learned how to handle.

"Thank you for listening," he settled on at last. "And for believing me."

"Thank you for telling me."

"I'm glad I did."

"How are you feeling?"

"Better, much better." Fier closed his eyes and let out a long, settling sigh. "You can go to sleep now, if you want."

"Are you sure?"

"Yes."

"Will you sleep?"

Could he sleep? Did he need to sleep? Since Fier had first awoken, the beast had chased him into unconsciousness; he had never fallen asleep without its intervention. Without the monster hounding him, would he just lie awake on the floor until sunrise? Or, for the first time in three years, would he be able to sleep in peace?

"If I can," he ceded eventually.

"Do you want me to stay awake with you?"

"No, angel. Go to sleep."

"Wake me if you need anything."

"I will."

"Good." The blankets rustled as Petra settled himself in, but the ensuing silence lasted only a moment before Petra broke it with a whispered "Fier?"

"Yes?"

"If it helps to know, I don't want to touch you that way." A rasp against the barn coat as Petra turned to look at him. "I don't want to touch anyone that way. I never have."

Fier bit the inside of his lip and resolutely said nothing. He stared at the ceiling, at the crack in the plaster he could barely see, and said nothing.

"You don't have to believe me, but that's the truth."

"Okay."

If Petra noticed how thinly-stretched Fier's voice was, he did not mention it. "Good night," was all he said, followed by a soft, "Sleep well."

Fier swallowed and listened to a further shuffle of blankets as Petra rolled to face the wall. The gardener's breathing, already smooth and slow, filled the room with a peace the manor had not housed all day. And beside him, Fier gave in at last, and fell, and fell, and fell.

Petra

PETRA WOKE TO BIRDSONG AND SUN. Just beyond his nose, the gleam of glass resolved itself into the scuffed impromptu vase as upright and half-full of water as Petra had left it the night before. Its fully-bloomed resident glowed orange in the sunrise, the gold at its heart as bright as a new star.

He sat up, shrugging off the now-tangled nest of blankets. His shoulder ached from where it had dug into the unyielding wood of the floor, and he rotated his arm with a wince as he turned to search the rest of the room for Fier.

He did not have to look far. The prince sat cross-legged beside his bed, gazing up at the coral sky beyond the window. Far from panicked, far from pained, he seemed calm, absolutely so, his shoulders loose and his hands open in his lap. As Petra tried to twist out the kink in his shoulder, Fier's attention snagged, and the prince favored him with such a bright and honest smile that Petra felt an identical one tugging at his own mouth.

"Did you sleep?"

"I did. Not a single bad dream."

"Good. You'll never have one again."

Fier's eyes were a clear bottle-green. "I've been thinking about that, Petra, and if you insist on being here at night to keep the beast away, I can't ask you to visit me day *and* night. It's not fair of me to expect or ask that of you. Not when you have a life beyond this."

Still warm, still hazy with sleep, Petra's first instinct was to protest. Fier had no one else to visit him, and time spent with him was not time wasted. But Fier was right: Petra *did* have responsibilities outside. By the end of summer, with the autumn harvests and preparations for winter beginning in earnest, he would have more still. He could not spend morning, noon, and night sequestered away here.

"Every night, then," he promised. "I'll be here before dark. No matter what."

"You were busy yesterday."

He had all but forgotten the fog and the rabbit, but they surged back into his thoughts in a confused muddle: the jumble of bone and fur, the singing, the relentless slam of his heart against his slowly-freezing chest.

"There was a rabbit." As usual, words felt inadequate, too shallow. "She was stuck. I had to figure out how to get her free."

Fier tilted his head so far to one side that his ear almost touched his shoulder. "Out of a snare, you mean?"

"No, out of her body."

"You didn't kill her?"

"She was already dead." Petra frowned, not sure how to explain the happenings to Fier, to himself. "Her spirit was stuck. Bottled up. She was buried with... shame, the first time, I think, and so we had to bury her again with... with sorrow, I guess. Respect. A genuine apology."

Fier studied him with his head still canted to one side, curious but clearly not in the least bit unsettled. "So you *are* a witch."

"I guess so."

"Marvelous. I wish I could have seen you."

Come with me, then. But Fier had already shied away from the prospect of venturing outside, and Petra would not put him through that again. "Marvelous or not," he said instead, "I'd rather not do it again any time soon. And I *will* be here before dark."

Fier favored him with another smile for that, but Petra avoided his eye by bundling up the blankets he had slept on. He rose to reorder them on the bed, and

Fier, like a shadow, likewise stood and followed just behind.

"You don't have to do that," he protested, bouncing on his toes at Petra's shoulder. "You can leave them on the floor if you want."

"I won't leave you with a mess." Petra straightened the corners on the first blanket, and began to fold the rest, one by one, at the foot of the bed. "This isn't my house."

"It's as much yours as it is mine. We're sharing."

"Then I'm doing my share of the chores."

Fier made a face, but did not protest further, and Petra retrieved his coat and boots without a word. He set the flower in its jar on the bedside table, but when he began to unwind the witch's pendant from the glass, he hesitated, and Fier darted forward at once:

"Take it," he insisted. "I won't need it."

But Petra still hesitated. "You *will* be alright while I'm gone?"

"Yes. It only comes after dark." Even when he wasn't smiling, Fier seemed lit from within. "I promise – I'll be fine."

- - -

For the first time, as he crossed the grounds back to the cottage, Petra glanced over his shoulder at the manor. He could see, high up against one of the third floor windows, a smudge of red and gold. It waved, and Petra waved back. As he turned to continue his course, he touched the strip of leather cord at his collar.

Be good, be brave, be kind. He could do that.

A dragonfly whirred past his ear, then wobbled through the air to skim over the surface of the nearest pond. The birds that had woken him with their music flashed past in streaks of blue and yellow. Flowers bloomed on all sides in summer profusion: thin green stems with tidy rows of blue-tinged bells, soft pink stars with leaves threaded gold, tiny purple florets tucked in among lancing emerald leaves.

Would Fier be bored? If Petra brought him new books, Fier would not be able to turn the pages, but he would at least have something new to look at. Perhaps he would like potted flowers – a garden for his room since he would not venture into the one outside. There was no way Petra could leave music for him, but maybe he could arrive in time to play the piano with him before the sun went down.

Lost in thought, Petra rounded the corner of the cottage and stumbled. He caught his balance, barely, but his legs gave out and he had to sit down, anyway, upon seeing what he had stumbled over.

Baskets and baskets and baskets covered the front step and part of the path beyond, all of them un-lidded and overflowing with old coats and blankets and fruit and bread and tiny pots of honey. Petra could see vegetables, strings of dried herbs, boots, folded sheets of fabric in fawn and earthen green. Even all of the townsfolks' previous gifts added together did not match this outpouring of gratitude on the steps of his home.

You worried everyone, Eckhart had said. Not *of* him – *for* him.

You worried everyone, Eckhart had said, and Petra, overwhelmed, not sure whether to laugh or cry, buried his face in his hands.

Fier

IN THE ABSENCE OF A PROPER THRONE ROOM, Eckhart had rearranged the dining room to serve instead. Between mealtimes, she cleared the table of the tablecloth and candles and, with Fier's high-backed chair alone at the head, removed all other seats but for three clustered at the far end of the table.

Seated in the chair opposite his own, Fier's current petitioner sat with an easy confidence and poise that Fier had long since given up trying to emulate. Hers were the broad shoulders and strong arms of someone whose livelihood was heavy work, and she wore her hair twisted in a straightforward, coffee-brown braid intended more for convenience than grandeur, though the result was the same.

Flanking her in the other two chairs were a pair of her younger farmhands, each of them well into their thirties and as sturdy as their superior. Fier, who had lingered often enough on the periphery of his parents' reception hall, had never seen petitioners so calm and confident.

"Good morning, Your Grace." The central petitioner dipped her head in formal greeting, then began without further preamble: "There has been an unfamiliar weed cropping up in the northern fields. As far as we can tell, it's not poisonous to us or our livestock, but even after we pull up the roots, anything growing nearby withers and dies. We've lost an acre of barley already."

Fier traced the curling vines carved into the arm of his chair and wished again, in vain, for paper and ink. Eckhart had forbidden both: "Taking notes looks unprofessional, Fier. If you would like a written record, I can transcribe the proceedings for you." But Fier had declined, afraid that the constant writing would make the visitors uneasy, and so Eckhart stood behind his right shoulder with her hands clasped behind her back and her expression, presumably, politely blank.

"So if Your Grace would be so kind," the farmer concluded, "you will provide us with some direction."

Watched by three sets of unblinking eyes, Fier resisted the urge to fidget or kick his heels or twist his hands together in his lap. "I don't--" he began, then broke off to speak more slowly, more carefully. "I am afraid I don't know enough about farming practices to properly advise you. Is there anyone else you can ask? An... an expert?"

The woman's expression did not change. "Your Grace has no immediate advice?" she asked, with a dismissive, falsely-surprised tone that sounded a great deal like those of the tutors Fier had left behind in the capital. "You don't want to study it or see it for yourself? Try to corral its growth?"

"You would know better than I how to handle this." Nerves were a sickening twist in the pit of his stomach, but Fier held his voice steady. "I will not give you false advice."

The farmhands' eyes skated toward their matron, and the woman rose with another formal nod. "Thank you, Your Grace." The farmhands rose, too, and the trio strode from the room, and Fier immediately clasped his hands, running the thumb of one hand over the fingertips of the other. The pressure settled his racing heart – only slightly, but enough.

Behind him, Eckhart shifted, just enough to draw his attention, and Fier tilted his head back to frown up at her. "What this time?"

The knight's expression was indeed one of blank politeness. "You should have taken control of the problem."

"What would you have me do? Lie? Pretend to

know what I don't?"

"No, Fier, but you should have taken it upon yourself to make further inquiries."

"Why? They know everyone who lives here. I don't. They would know the most qualified person to ask. I don't. They know how to handle the problems associated with crops. I don't."

Eckhart sighed, as she had been doing with an increasing frequency these last few months, and her disappointment dampened Fier's rising hysteria – and his confusion, his dismay, and everything else besides. What did any of this matter, anyway? The town had thrived without him, and it would thrive after he left. He was only here so that he could be more easily ignored by his family.

"We will try again, Fier," Sir Eckhart promised, but Fier dropped his gaze to the polished tabletop. "You will learn – you *are* learning."

- - -

"He says the foal is his since it keeps crossing into his garden, but I know for a fact my jennet is the mother."

Fier sat with his arms crossed over his chest and only his respect for Sir Eckhart kept him from propping his feet on the edge of the table. Seated at the far end of the dining room, the two men supposedly fighting over the newborn donkey had put two chairs side by side and sat with their shoulders touching.

"Kill it."

Behind him, just visible out of the corner of his eye, Eckhart flinched. One of the farmers blanched. The other leaned forward as if afraid he had misheard. His voice, though politely quiet, carried easily across the total silence of the dining room: "Excuse me, Your Grace?"

"You heard me. Kill it. Cut it in half. Right down the middle. You can each have half."

"Oh. Well. Your Grace, don't you think it might be better if--"

"No." Fier's stomach churned not with nerves (never, now, with nerves), but with the molten tangle of indignation and annoyance rooted there since breakfast. "You asked me for advice, and now you have it."

"But we could--"

"If you already had your solution," Fier interceded, "as you *always* do, why did you ask for my assistance? Thank you and good-bye."

The two farmers stood with a care that belied their continued surprise and turned to leave. As they stepped from the room, still side by side, Fier felt Eckhart set her hand on the high, carved back of his chair.

"That's enough for today, Your Grace," she

whispered, and her tone was still, somehow, impossibly patient. "That's enough."

That's enough.

That's enough.

That's enough.

Fier blinked – and blinked again. A sliver of moonlight left a swathe of silver-edged shadows across the bedroom. On the nightstand sat the jar, the glass bright and pearlescent, its glow banded by the dark crisscross of Petra's leather cord. The flower leaned against the rim, as unmolested tonight as it had been for the last two weeks.

No nightmares anymore. Just memories.

Fier lay on the floor, his back to the closed door, but unease stirred in his chest and he sat up. Beside him, between him and the door, on the mattress pulled from the bed and wrapped in borrowed blankets, Petra still lay sleeping.

People were at their most innocent when they slept, and Petra was no different. He had pulled the blankets up to his chin and tucked his nose under a quilt-covered hand. He slept on his left side and his spilled-ink skin was just visible in the darkness, shadow within shadow. Petra had mostly stopped angling his head to hide the darker half of his face, but Fier could see a subtle, self-conscious tilt still happen when he sat at Petra's right.

The birthmark blocked off almost all his cheek like a continent on an antique map. The coast crossed over part of Petra's nose, briefly followed his cheekbone, caught the corner of his eye, and journeyed up his forehead to disappear past his hairline. In the other direction, the smudge crossed the last quarter of his mouth, and maybe that was part of why Petra was shy to smile. A tiny island over his eyebrow was the only mark isolated from the whole.

He *was* beautiful. Not in spite of his birthmark. The smudges were as much a part of Petra as his gentleness or his calf-brown eyes, and Fier loved the pieces as much as he loved the whole. Maybe *because* he loved the whole. Or maybe the other way around.

The unease Fier had felt upon waking kicked a notch higher, and he let his gaze be drawn to the closed bedroom door. He could see, in the moonlight, dark tendrils licking up beneath the door and curling back into the hallway beyond.

Petra stirred, disturbed, perhaps, by the same apprehensiveness. Fier watched the door, but he could hear the gardener's breathing hitch as he woke, could hear him roll over to face the door, could see him prop himself up on an elbow as if preparing to rise.

"It's alright," Fier promised. "It can't get in."

Petra said nothing, and they watched in mutual silence as the shadows struggled against the invisible barrier on their side of the door. Fier's skin prickled, and the feeling of disquiet lodged in his throat, but he left it there. It would pass. This would pass.

Eventually, the shadows slid back beneath the door and did not return. Petra let out the breath he had been holding, and the knots in Fier's chest and throat unraveled.

"Fier? Are you okay?"

"Yes."

"Good." Petra resettled himself on the mattress, his arms folded over the mused blankets and his head tipped so he could look up at Fier. "Has it done that before?"

Fier shrugged, though he doubted Petra could see him very well in the dark. "I don't know," he admitted. "If so, it's not woken me before."

"How long have you been awake?"

"Just a few minutes. But you should go back to sleep. You have all those potatoes to dig up tomorrow."

"If you can't sleep, I'll stay awake with you."

"I'll sleep. I *will*," he added with a laugh as Petra's mouth tilted into a disbelieving frown. "I promise, Petra. Get your rest."

"I don't like leaving you awake by yourself."

"You need your sleep. That comes first."

Reluctant, obviously so, Petra slowly tucked himself back under the blankets and pulled them up over his nose. Fier lay beside him, too far to reach, his arm a pillow against his cheek. Petra watched him, as if expecting him to sit up again, but Fier made no move to do so.

There was so much trust wrapped up in sleeping beside someone: trust that they would not see vulnerability as an advantage, trust that they would not hurt. How Petra could fall asleep so easily? Even as Fier watched, the gardener's eyes fluttered closed, and his breath softened, as if he thought nothing of shared sleeping space.

Not until he was certain that Petra was truly and deeply asleep did Fier roll onto his back and close his eyes. He missed, a little, mattresses and pillows and the enveloping warmth of blankets, but for now, the wooden floor caused him no discomfort, and he might have been aware, painfully aware, of Petra's presence beside him had there not been a rift between them much wider than the arm-span between them.

- - -

True to form, he was the first to wake the next morning. Petra rose shortly after, awakened by the first rays of the new sun, and Fier trailed after him as he tidied away his makeshift bed ("You *know* you can leave all that on the floor, Petra,") and unwound his pendant in preparation to return to his life outside.

But Petra paused there, stood arrested with the

jar in one hand and the pendant in the other. He ran his thumb over the stone with such a puzzled crease between his eyebrows that Fier bounced up beside him to see what had caught him so.

"It feels different," Petra explained, answering Fier's unasked question. "I think the hole is bigger."

Fier could see no difference. The stone was still small and grey and unremarkable, with its punch of a hole through the middle, but Petra had worn it every day for the last nine years: Petra alone would know if the shape of it had changed.

"It *is* a stone. A little wear won't hurt it."

"I suppose so." Petra set down Fier's flower and, with both hands, looped the cord over his head and tucked the pendant under his shirt.

"Will it be safe for you to come back tonight?"

"Of course."

"Good! Enjoy digging up all those potatoes." Fier lifted his gaze from the pendant to Petra, met his eyes from beneath a fringe of dark lashes. "And tell everyone that I think you're handsome."

Petra almost-smiled at that – there was a tiny twist at the corners of his mouth – but when Fier returned the smile tenfold, Petra gave in and pulled the collar of his shirt over his nose to hide his mouth.

"I will," he promised, his smile audible in his voice. "Dig up the potatoes, at least."

Petra

PETRA HAD FOLDED HIS COAT on the tilled earth behind him and worked, for the first time in company,
with his sleeves rolled nearly to his elbows. His eyes
kept catching on the mottled skin plainly visible
across his fingers and palms and all the way up both
arms, but seeing them – and knowing that others
could see them – did nothing to dim the sun alight in
his chest. With the summer day unclouded and blinding, Petra felt as warm inside as out.

The bed of dense, heart-shaped leaves turned
almost white in the sun. The vines twisted together so
tightly that only the yellow edges marked where one
plant ended and another began. Everyone but Sir
Eckhart worked out of Petra's periphery, and Petra
noticed them only for their music, for the rustle of
vines gathered in armloads and their combined voices
more like the wind than shared words.

On his left, Eckhart dug up sweet potatoes with

the aid of a two-pronged gardening fork, but Petra, as always, preferred to use his bare hands. The potatoes grew so close to the surface that he could dip just his fingertips into the soil and touch them. Collecting each one was a ceremony: a tangle of vines eased away, hands pressed palm-flat against the soil, a gentle recovery from the earth, the clinging dirt dusted from burnt-orange skin. Petra set each in the basket beside his folded coat, mindful of the ease with which they bruised.

"You seem cheerful."

"I am." Petra pushed a handful of vines back from their roots and nudged a dark, glossy beetle back under the cover of the foliage. But even with Eckhart watching him, Petra could not fight the buoyancy that started in his toes and rose through his chest and ended in a smile as impossible to hide as the marks on his cheek.

"Is there a cause?" Eckhart rested the gardening fork on her knee. "More unexpected gifts?"

"Yes." *Handsome*. Fier thought him *handsome*.

"Do you need help sorting through them again?"

"Not this time. Thank you."

Eckhart nodded and returned to her work, but Petra remained motionless for a minute longer and tried to come down from the clouds. He should have been worried. The stone pendant was wearing away, the shadow creature had nearly breached the door, he had yet to see Fier *actually* get any rest, and Petra had been too distracted upon leaving the manor that morning to remember to eat breakfast. Fier had complimented him before, many times before, so why had this one left him glowing?

But, as the same glossy black beetle trundled out of the potato vines and marched up Petra's arm, Petra knew why.

Iris had always talked about love like it was a lightning strike – something sharp and searing and unpredictable, something that tore its victim in half. But Petra had always thought of love as a fire: a small and wavering flame that needed to be coaxed, that grew only with time and care and kindling. Lightning, with all its violence, was there then gone, but a fire flickered and grew and faded, strong or weak by turns.

And love was everywhere. Petra harbored lit candles even for strangers, their wicks burning small and steady and self-contained. Candles were as natural as an indrawn breath. But the strongest fires, those kindled for the hearth – those were born from a conscious decision to breathe sparks to warmer life, to lay kindling for the flickering embers in the fireplace. As long as there was kindling enough and time enough and care enough, those fires would last. Love would last.

And in recalling the sunlit edges of Fier's uninhibited smile, Petra knew there, at least, was kindling enough.

He pulled at the pendant's leather cord with two fingers, running the worn length of it against his thumb. "Sir?" he asked, turning askance to Eckhart. "May I ask you something?"

The knight rocked back on her heels and rested the gardening fork on her knee again.

"What happened when you went in after Fier?"

Eckhart's expression did not change, but she set the fork down in the dirt. "I went blind," she replied, matter-of-fact. "Not at first. None of the lamps remained lit inside, so I could hardly see anyway, but five steps in, I went blind. I tried to reach the ballroom, and I kept calling for Fier, but I'd been turned around: I stumbled out the front door instead."

"Were you afraid?"

"Yes. But that was not enough to keep me from trying."

"What kept you from trying again?"

Eckhart was slower to answer that. She studied the stretch of sun-bright leaves without seeing them, tracing two fingers along the bone of her cheek. "I thought Fier didn't want to be found," she began, almost to herself.

"I thought the beast might be there to protect him. That paralysis that stopped everyone just past the doors, some people thought that was a sign of the prowling beast, a way for it to still its prey, but I don't think so.

"Fier was afraid that night. He had been afraid for a long time. I should have seen that sooner than I did. So much sooner. He wanted to hide – from me, from everyone. He's hiding now, and I won't try to pull him out if he's not ready."

Petra had forgotten about the beetle; it bumped against his neck. Absently, he plucked it from his collar. "So you couldn't go back in," he mused, releasing the insect back in among the potato vines, "but you never left."

"Of course not. Fier is my responsibility. He is my family. He is here, so I will stay. And you," she added, almost as an afterthought. "You were generous and trusting and, after Nadeen and Iris, alone. Someone had to keep an eye on you."

Petra toyed with one of the sweet potato leaves, its heart-shape flaring as he pulled at one edge. "He's sorry. He wanted me to tell you that."

"He told you what happened?"

"He said he struck you."

"Then you know he has nothing to apologize for. The fault is mine."

With that, Eckhart picked up the gardening fork again and turned back to her work, and Petra knew he should have let the conversation drop, but, "I don't think he can sleep," he blurted out instead, and when Eckhart looked at him, he hastened through the rest: "When I fall asleep, he's still awake. He's awake whenever I wake up, even in the middle of the night."

"That sounds like him." Eckhart's voice was so soft it barely reached him. "He wouldn't go to sleep if I or anyone else was in the room. He became more... vehement about it as he grew up, but when he was a child, he'd fall asleep anywhere, sometimes even in the parlor. Twelve adults discussing politics and there he would be: fast asleep, curled in a chair. I'd have to carry him to bed."

Again, Eckhart turned back to the sweet potatoes, and Petra did not call her attention away. He retrieved the pendant from beneath his shirt, traced the shape of it with the pad of his thumb, and felt again the sliver of unease that came with finding its dimensions changed. The hole was definitely wider, noticeably so, and there was a thin, hairline crack radiating from the center to the perimeter that had not been present that morning.

Whether by fluke or by design, the pendant's magic was fading. But whenever the magic failed altogether, and whatever followed after, Petra would be

ready for it. Here, with the heartbeat of the earth puls-
ing in his hands and in the soles of his feet, with *I
think you're handsome* a ringing echo all through his
chest, he could do anything.

Petra

PETRA WOKE, disoriented, to total darkness. He blinked, momentarily blind in the overcast, moonless night, and tried to marshal his thoughts enough to pinpoint what had woken him. He could hear nothing beyond the gentle sheeting of rain outside, and there was no prickle of fear in his chest that accompanied the attempted nightly visits of the shadow.

"Petra?" Fier's voice from behind him, barely above a whisper but spoken with an insistence that suggested repetition. "Are you awake?"

"Yes." He began to roll over, to face the speaker, but the tone of the prince's voice arrested him partway; he'd heard that hitch in Fier's breath often enough to know what it meant. The sound hooked him fully awake and "Yes," he said again, more certain this time. "What's wrong?"

"Nothing. I just..." Fier trailed off, and Petra waited, hardly breathing in case he missed Fier's answer, until the prince began again, nearly impossible to hear over the rain: "When did you know that... that you didn't like... certain things?"

Petra hesitated, then suggested, equally quiet, "The 'bedroom stuff,' you mean?"

"Yeah."

"Always, I guess. I always knew."

"How?"

Petra shrugged, realized too late that Fier probably could not see him in the dark. "Iris, mostly," he admitted. "She tried to convince me to give sex and all of that a chance. I couldn't see the appeal. I wasn't interested. I told her so."

"Did she believe you?"

"She didn't understand, but she left me alone." Kissing, he remembered, had been the only part she had been adamant that he try, and Petra could still recall how deeply he had dug in his heels against her persuasion. "I wasn't going to change my mind."

For a long moment, Fier said nothing. Petra's eyes began to adjust to the lack of light, and he could pick out the frame of the bed, the edge of the window. When Fier did finally speak, it was a low, barely audible, "Oh."

Petra did, then, turn to face Fier. He could identify the curve of his shoulder, the curve of the arm pillowing his head. "I'm sorry no one did that for you. I'm sorry no one listened to you."

Fier said nothing; Petra could see him loop an arm around his waist, draw his legs up as if to curl in on himself.

"You said no, Fier. And you kept saying no. They should have left you alone. They should have stopped trying to touch you."

"They didn't understand."

"You said no. That's all they had to understand."

Again, Fier said nothing, only pulled himself into a smaller shape in the darkness, and, again, Petra felt the urge to soothe with contact, to press *you're okay, you're safe, you did nothing wrong* against hand or arm or cheek. But touch was not wanted, and was impossible besides, and Petra let the urge rise and fall away.

"You shouldn't have to do anything except say no," he said instead. "The best you can do is stay away from the ones who don't listen, if you can. No matter who they are."

"I don't like hands on my neck."

"Oh." The statement had the weight of a confession, and Petra hesitated, uncertain of what was expected from him. "I-- Okay."

"Or my waist."

"Okay."

"Except as part of a hug, then it's alright." A

shift in the shadows: Fier twisting to look at him instead of at the floor. "What about you?"

"Me?"

An exhale – a laugh or a sigh. "Yes, *you*."

Petra drew his half-forgotten blanket up to his chin, then over his nose. Homesickness surged in his chest and closed his throat. Nadeen was gone, and so the hand ruffling his hair, the back against his at night, the shoulder brushing his during work in the garden – those, too, were gone. Iris was gone, and so the elbow looped through his, the playful walk of fingers along his wrist, the arms around his waist in a sudden hug from behind – those, too, were gone.

"I think," he began, trying to gauge what, if anything, had been unwelcome, "I think as long as it's innocent, I'm alright."

"Hugs?" Fier pressed. "Hugs are innocent?"

"Yes."

"And holding hands?"

"Yes."

"Good." Another exhale, this one definitely a sigh. "That's good."

"Fier?"

"Yes?"

I'd like that with you. But that was not wanted, had not been asked for. "Are you okay?"

"Yes." As close as Fier had been to tears when

Petra woke, he sounded reassuringly far from them now. "Yes, I am alright. Good night, Petra."

Petra let the silence stretch for a moment longer, but Fier said nothing else, and the tap of rain was the only sound between them. "Good night," he conceded, and, with Fier a dark, still shape on the rug beside him, closed his eyes and tried to settle back into sleep.

Fier

WITH THE SUN GONE from the high windows and the piano keys lit only by the golden glow of the lantern propped against the music rack, the ballroom felt smaller and more private than it had ever been in Fier's lifetime.

The low light gave Petra some difficulty, and he played as slowly and carefully as he had during their first sessions, but Fier had played this before, over and over and over again, and he knew his own part so well he no longer needed to look at the keys. He watched Petra's hands instead of his own, then slowed to match his tempo.

Even slow, even a little dissonant, Fier fell into the sweep of music, relaxed into the push and pull of sound, of stepping almost-smoothly from one note to the next. The piano keys felt cold and beautifully solid at his touch; Petra's shoulder was a fabric whisper against his own.

Petra missed a note, then another, and, embarrassed, withdrew from the keys. With an intentional misstep, Fier missed one of his own to call him back. But Petra had lost the thread, and he had lost the placement of his hands, and he would not play. Fier gave up the melody entirely and let the last note echo to nothing in the wide, empty room. He nudged Petra with his elbow – a rasp of sleeve against coat.

"Keep going," he prompted. "Play anything."

Petra glanced at him, and Fier offered a reassuring smile. "Play anything," he prompted again. "It's not a duet without you."

With the dimpled beginnings of a smile, Petra did play – one lonely, ringing note. Fier danced around it, buoyed it up into the start of a new song, and as Petra played a second, and a third, Fier matched him again, this time with accompaniment written nowhere but in the space between them.

Petra stumbled into a melody and kept it, and Fier played a countermelody, until Petra played nothing but the same four notes over and again, and, thus prompted, Fier swept in to lead with a tune light and fast and exuberant, and their combined efforts were messy and clumsy and new, but Petra's smile was in earnest now, and Fier laughed to see it, and it was Petra's turn to nudge Fier's shoulder —

Fier woke with a start. To a bedroom shadowed

by light from a waxing moon. To Petra beside him. To the ringing echoes of their shared composition already a dream fading, fading, gone.

Autumn had begun to turn the evenings frigid, and Petra slept beneath blankets both from Fier's room and from his own cottage on the grounds. He looked the same at rest as he did every night: soft, serene, ethereal in the moonlight. He kept one hand tucked beneath his cheek, but the other rested palm-up beside him on the pillow: his right hand, the spilled-ink of his skin nearly invisible; his silver, star-lit fingers curled above the shadowed pool of a palm.

Fier untucked his arm from around his own waist and, soundless, bodiless, touched the nearest of Petra's fingertips. But this was not a dream, and his gloved hand passed through Petra's bare one.

He traced the curve of Petra's palm anyway, down to his wrist and then back up along the curl of his smallest finger. He spread his fingers and ghosted his palm against Petra's. When he closed his hand, his fingers passed through Petra's; he felt the press of them against his own palm instead.

He touched, or attempted to touch, Petra's forehead, to brush back the curl of his hair, touching so lightly he could imagine that his was not the insubstantial touch of a ghost. He traced a finger along the straight line of Petra's nose. Drew a line along the curve of Petra's cheek.

But Petra shifted, hunched his shoulder against a cold Fier could not feel, and Fier forgot for a moment that he could do nothing. He reached for the topmost blanket to pull it up to Petra's cheek, and his hand, of course, passed through the fabric. Petra burrowed beneath the covers on his own, and stilled.

Morning was still a long way off, but Fier rose anyway and went to sit by the window. He pulled his knees to his chest and looked out at the gardens, at the cascade of moonlit flowers and star-silvered leaves tousled by a breeze he could not feel.

Petra

After Nadeen and Iris, Petra had always found the gatekeeper's cottage to be too big and too empty, even with its tumult of greenery, and Petra was at a loss to pinpoint when, precisely, in the last few weeks, that had changed.

Eckhart had helped him put up more shelves, but even so, there was hardly enough room. Pots of honey and preserves crowded jars of dried witch hazel, willow bark, star anise, and chips of sandalwood. The jars of spindly mint and parsley on the windowsill shared their precious square of sunlight with growing green onions and lacy swathes of white flowers. Herbs hung from the rafters in a forest of thyme and sage and dandelion. The only table, low and scarred and smooth with use, still hosted a cluster of cups brimming with seeds and new sprouts; bowls were scattered between, full of bread and the last of the summer vegetables. A crate tucked behind the half-barrel of wildly-blooming heather housed more old coats and boots than he had ever owned before, and his sleeping mat hosted so many blankets that it very nearly resembled a proper bed.

Petra sat against these now, the last of the day's light pooling gold in the doorway. He cradled the witch's pendant in his hand and ran his thumb along what was left of it.

"Are there more cracks in it?" Fier had asked that morning.

"None yet," Petra had answered, and that had been Petra's answer for the last several days. "It won't break yet."

"If you're sure. I don't want you hurt."

"It won't break yet."

But Petra was no longer certain that the pendant would last through the night. It had been steadily crumbling over the course of the day and now only a paper-thin ring of stone remained. The hole had eaten away the rest. Though thin, stone was stone; it should not have felt so fragile, as if even the smallest pressure would—

Tck.

Petra felt the split before he heard it, but even then, he did not at once register what was meant by the two cracked halves in his hand. Despite the blankets, despite his coat, he sat frozen.

This was it, then. The magic was gone. The protection was gone.

Fear closed over Petra's heart, and for a moment, he considered staying in the cottage. He could wait until sunrise to visit Fier. He could explain what had happened. He could show him the broken halves of the pendant.

But he was already standing, staring still at the broken pendant, already walking toward the cottage door, already crossing the threshold. He closed the door behind him, closed his hand over the stone. He would go. He would *always* go – tonight and tomorrow and every day after.

The sun hung orange and gold on the horizon, but Petra felt none of its last heat. Long shadows stretched across the grass, and Petra's own wavered beside him on the garden path. He did not stop for fresh water this time. He had forgotten the flask and he did not know, if he paused, if he would be able to keep going before nightfall.

He might go blind. He might be killed. He might arrive too late to keep the beast from Fier, if he even could keep it away. He might be powerless to stop the beast from attacking the flower or from drowning Fier in a storm of panic.

But Petra did not like – had never liked – how fear curdled the impulse to be kind. He was going inside.

Come what may, he was going inside. He would not leave Fier to face the beast alone.

Standing before the fully-closed front door, Petra reached for the leather cord at his neck and, of course, found his throat bare. The sunset painted the door crimson.

With an exhale, Petra wrenched open the door and crossed the threshold. The thicker, heavier air caught in his lungs as it always did, and for one gasp, Petra could not breathe. Fear clamped around his heart like a vice, and Petra squeezed the broken pendant so tightly that it fractured in his hand; stone dust trickled between his fingers.

Your feet are on the ground, Nadeen had said. *You are here.* Here in the same foyer, with the same shrouded mirror and the same dustless table, that he had walked through countless times before.

Petra did not move yet. He exhaled again, and the next breath came easier, and the next after. The knot of fear did not lessen, but Petra had not expected it to. If he had to carry that with him, so be it. He could be afraid and still walk forward.

His heart hammered so hard he could feel it in his throat and in his palms, but Petra took one step forward. A second. A third. He wanted to leave – to turn and run – so much so that his legs felt like string, but more than that, with a fierceness and a fire stronger than the crushing panic, he wanted to keep going. Fier felt a fear this deep every time the shadow touched him, and Petra would not leave him to face that alone.

With each step, he expected blindness – or pain – or the swell of the shadow-beast itself. But each step brought nothing except the echoing *thmp* of his boots against the wooden floor, the sound painfully loud in the wide and empty rooms.

He found the ballroom dark and cold – a cave without any last streaks of sunlight. He found the banister of the arching staircase, wound his way up to the floor above. His pulse was rabbit-fast, and Petra could feel it all down his arms, could feel his heart stuttering in his chest. But he grit his teeth and followed the flight of stairs up once more to the third and final landing. Fier's door had been left ajar – Petra had left it so that morning – and a faint glow to the hall floor was all that remained of the day's light.

There was no time left to linger in the hall. Petra dug the heel of his closed hand into his chest and stumbled forward. He could not breathe as easily as he had before, could almost not breathe at all. Dizzy, his legs almost too weak to hold him up, he kept his other hand on the wall for balance and inched, painfully slow, down the corridor.

He reached Fier's doorway and leaned against

the threshold. His heart was beating so loud and with such force that he wanted it to stop. This was so hard. This was too much.

Fier stood at the window, his hair lit scarlet by the last shard of sunlight. The flower was propped unharmed in the jar on the bedside table. Fier stood on his tip-toes beside it, peering anxiously down at the grounds below. Looking for him. Expecting him.

"Fier." Petra could barely hear himself over the thud of his pulse in his ears. "I'm here."

"Petra!" Fier spun and bounded toward him at once. "I was starting to—Oh! What's wrong? What happened?"

Petra did not have the breath to answer. Slowly, with an unreasonable effort, he pulled his hand away from his chest and uncurled his fingers. The pendant had almost been crushed entirely to dust, but small shards of stone still glinted in the grey sand.

"No." Fier's green eyes flashed from the dust to Petra's face. "*Petra.*"

Petra tried to shake his head, managed a faded, near-soundless, "I'm here."

"Petra, *please*. Look at you. You have to *go*."

Not without you. But Petra couldn't speak, could barely think, hadn't planned anything beyond this, beyond being here when the shadow came for Fier. Fier wouldn't be alone. No matter what else happened, Fier wouldn't be alone.

"It's *killing* you." Fier stepped closer and pushed his hands through Petra's chest as if to shove him back into the hallway. There was a *thump* from behind Fier as the flower writhed in its jar and tumbled onto the rug. Fier didn't seem to notice. "You can't--" His voice cracked, split into a hiccup of panic. "You can't be here, Petra, you *can't.*"

Petra's grip slackened. What was left of the pendant fell in a swathe of dust from his palm.

Beyond the glass of the window, the sun slipped at last out of sight.

The hairs on the back of Petra's neck rose, and Fier's eyes, bright and sharp, caught on something in the hall behind him.

"*No,*" Fier hissed. He hunched forward – a shield, curled his arms around – through – Petra's shoulders. "You will *not* touch him."

Petra turned, sick and dizzy with the movement – doubly so upon seeing the creature. The beast more hole than shape, its drooping head without eyes or mouth or nose. Arms, stringy and melting, formed out of the void of its body.

As fast as a blink, the creature lurched forward – and more with instinct than plan, Petra stumbled into its path, wedged himself between the shadow and the room – between the shadow and the flower – between the shadow and Fier.

The rest was a jumble: Fier shouting again, surging forward to shield him again; a streak of red and glowing gold; the flower coiling on the rug, twisting with new roots and new leaves and shattering the jar as it grew too big and fast to hold; "*No!* You *will not* touch him!"

The shadow wrapped around Fier, and then around Petra, and with another cry from Fier, this one of pain, Petra's heart stalled and the world fell away.

Fier

STARS. Fier had never seen so many stars.

He had always never seen so many stars.

He was done with stars.

He dropped his gaze from the dizzy swirl and scanned the rest of the scene instead: the dancing couples in masks and velvet, the wooden arches scattered with paper lanterns. The silhouette of the manor looming over all, each of its windows lit from within by a flickering, pale yellow glow.

Movement on the ground drew his eye: a flower blooming in the grass at his ankle, the whole of it as small as a pearl, its buttery petals fanning outward in delicate curves even as Fier watched. Another bloomed at its hip – and another, and another – and then a cluster all at once, bursting into life under the feet of the dancing couples until a carpet of soft gold swept across the whole of the once-barren lawn.

Petra.

A copper mask bent into the muzzle and mane of a lion. A laugh tinkling like broken glass. A hand sought his, pulled him into a dance. A second found his shoulder.

"Eyes on me, Your Grace."

"Where's Petra?"

"Who?"

"*Petra.*"

"He's not here."

Fier dug in his heels and tried to yank his hand out of his partner's grasp. She slowed to a stop, but her grip was as strong a cage as iron and she did not let go.

"You're lying to me."

"He's not here."

"Let me go."

"All hands, Your Grace." Her fingertips crept up the back of his neck, and Fier hunched his shoulders, froze at the cold, stomach-twisting shock of contact. "He will be no different."

Nausea crept up the back of his throat and coiled in his stomach. But Fier had been frightened already, had been frantic already, and there was more in him than fear. Lightning and monsoon winds coursed through his bloodstream and all he could see was Petra unsteady in his doorway, his face grey, his hand over his heart like it was cracking into pieces in his chest.

This place had lied to him. This place had hurt him. This place had stolen Petra, and Fier would tear it apart.

"I *know*," he began, teeth gritted against a rising, rising heat, "I *know* that you will *never* leave me alone. I *know* I'm stuck with you – until the day I die – but I will *not* let you take the rest of my life – and do not think – not for a *moment* – that you can take *him*."

"You have been wrong before, Your Grace. You will *always* be wrong."

"I trust *him*. I don't trust *you*."

She dug her fingernails into his skin. Fier's vision pulsed white-hot and he wrenched himself free, stumbled backward, turned and fled through the crowd. He could hear her tinkling laugh, but there was no swirl of grey smoke, no hook in the pit of his stomach to pull him awake, so Fier kept running, dodging dancing couples, tearing past wooden bowers with huge golden lilies curling up between the latticework. Petra had to be here. He *had* to be here.

White silk gowns, cloaks in scarlet and gold, masks in copper and silver and midnight lace. There were so many, so many, all of them spinning, twirling in a whirlwind of rich fabric and glittering jewels. Petra was here somewhere. He *had* to be.

And he *was*. There – an island of stillness among

so much motion, unmasked and dressed for gardening, studying the nearest dancers with a puzzled
frown, as out of place in this fairy court as a fern
among roses. Fier's heart raced and Fier raced with it.

Petra glanced up – saw him – turned toward
him – and without slowing, Fier threw his arms
around Petra's neck, crashed into him with such force
that Petra stumbled back a step. Fier closed his eyes
and buried his face against the collar of Petra's shirt,
and with a little huff of surprise that Fier felt against
the curve of his neck, Petra relaxed and wrapped his
arms around Fier's waist. Even here, Petra smelled
like earth and soil and sunlight, and Fier drew in a
deep, reverent breath.

He could still feel the shadow of her hand crawling up his neck, but stronger still was the cleansing
warmth of safe, beloved arms around him. Petra's embrace threatened to crush his ribs, but Fier tightened
his all the more and burrowed his face into Petra's
shoulder. Petra said nothing, and did not let him go,
and gradually Fier's heart caught the calmer beat of
Petra's and slowed, slowed, slowed to match.

"Fier?" Petra asked at last. "Are you alright?"

"Yes. Yes, if you are."

Another puff of warm air against his neck – a
soft, soundless sigh of relief. "Yes, I am, if *you* are."

Fier drew in one last, dizzying breath, then

loosened his grip, and the two of them broke apart. He could feel the embrace even after it ended, a welcome ghost, for once.

Half-afraid that Petra would vanish if he let go, Fier kept ahold of his sleeves, his fingers worked so tightly into the loose fabric that his fingertips were numb.

"I love you," he admitted, much belated. "Just so you know."

"I do know." Petra was smiling, had possibly been smiling the whole time, the crease of a dimple deep in one cheek. "I could see it."

"Good. I'm going to show you every day."

Petra didn't answer. He eased one of Fier's hands free and put up one of his own and carefully threaded their fingers together. Fier felt no jolt of surprise or delight, just the warm weight of a hand in his, the gentle pressure against his palm and between his fingers.

"You should have let me face that thing alone," Fier added in a whisper. "I thought... I thought you were dying."

The hand in his tightened – a fleeting press of reassurance. "I didn't."

"I thought you were dying."

"Fier, I didn't. I'm here. I'm with you."

"Why did you do that? Why did you come?"

Petra's laugh had weight – a shower of warm summer rain. "For the same reason I always visit you: I love you."

"Oh." Fier's heart lodged in his throat. *I love you.* "Oh. Petra, you love everyone."

"I do. But you get a bigger piece of my heart than most."

He could not bring himself to meet Petra's eye, so he stared at their joined hands instead, at the thin crescent of earth beneath Petra's fingernails, the heartbeat against his palm maybe his own, maybe Petra's, maybe both together.

"I want this." The words were out of Fier's mouth before he meant them to be. "What we have already – and this."

"'This?'"

"Just… just *this*," Fier managed. He could feel Petra looking at him, but he refused to look up, refused to wipe his eyes, refused, too, to acknowledge the hitch in his voice. "The… the innocent things. If that's alright. If that's enough."

"Fier." Petra tilted his head in an effort to catch Fier's eye, and when Fier ducked to hide his face, Petra gently swept his hair back from his forehead. "What we had was already enough. *This* will be enough. This is *more* than enough."

Fier did not – could not – answer, and, vision

blurred, he leaned forward and nudged his forehead against Petra's. Petra laughed, the same soft and delighted sigh from before, and slipped his hand from Fier's now-slack grip to brush both into Fier's hair – and nuzzled Fier back with such vehemence that Fier hiccupped a laugh and retreated.

"You *are* okay?" he asked. "You didn't get hurt?"

"I don't think so," was Petra's reply, and his smile eased. "Where are we?"

"In a bad dream." Fier skated a hand through his hair to straighten it after Petra's interference. "I think we should leave."

But Petra did not seem to be listening, and his smile had faded entirely. He reached up, caught Fier's arm, and gently drew it back down. Fier saw them, too: three long scratches across his wrist welling with blood, the cuts thin and shallow. Only now, as he noticed them, did they begin to sting; the back of his neck, too, began to ache.

"What hurt you?"

"A bad memory." Fier watched as Petra wiped away the blood with the end of his own sleeve. "A ghost."

"I don't like this place."

"Neither do I. I'm done with it."

"How do we leave?"

Though he had never made it this far into the

dream, had never successfully escaped from the talons of his lion-masked partner, Fier turned without
hesitation toward the manor standing sentinel behind
them. "We go in there."

"Have you done that before?"

"No."

"Alright."

Fier turned one palm up in the space between
them, and Petra took it, and they walked side-by-side
and hand-in-hand toward the manor and its other-
worldly glow. Fier laced their fingers together this
time, and as before, there was no jolt, no leap, no
flood of heat at the connection, just the welcome
warmth and security of a hand in his.

The masked dancers ignored them and, though
he looked at each couple they passed, he could not see
a lion mask among them. Flowers continued to grow
and bloom around them as they walked up the slight
incline of the lawn. Golden flowers already covered
the lawn from one corner to the last, but tiny white
blossoms flowered behind Petra in the wake of his
steps. Joining the lilies on the wooden arches were
dahlias as rich and dark a blue as the night sky, speckled with white flecks like stars.

As they reached the manor, Petra touched the
wall beside the door. Ivy twisted out from cracks in the
masonry, curled up and across the wall in a blanket of

five-pointed leaves; flowers bloomed among the leaves: bright, sun-yellow petals edged with a swirl of gold, their hearts a deep and mellow brown.

Fier ran one of the nearest leaves between his fingers. "This one is yours."

Petra studied the rambling vines, his beautiful two-toned face lit by the light of the manor's open door. "Like the one in the jar is yours?"

"Yes. And I was wrong before," Fier added with a burgeoning grin. "*This* one is my favorite."

Petra shook his head, but tugged up the collar of his shirt to hide his embarrassment. He tightened his hold on Fier's hand, and without further conversation, crushed close by the narrowness of the doorway, they stepped into the manor together.

They did not step into the foyer. They stepped into nothing at all, poised on the edge of a long stretch of empty hallway, the walls and floor and ceiling a void, the only light at all a distant pinprick at the end. Fier had not noticed the violins or the soft murmur of voices until both were abruptly gone, but when he glanced back over his shoulder, the doorway behind them had not vanished; he could see the gold and scarlet dancers, the sweep of flowers, the star-strewn night sky.

As he turned back to the hallway, the shape of it changed: the darkness of the walls hollowed and sharpened in turns, became slender tree trunks with branches interlocking overhead to become a new ceiling, a canopy dense with dark leaves. Moss and grass feathered the ground, and the floor underfoot swelled into the natural dip and curve of a deep-forest path.

As with the flowers outside, Petra could not make the dream disappear altogether, but – whether he knew it or not – he could make it less daunting.

"Fier." Petra's voice sounded strange and out of place in the unnatural silence. "This might break the curse."

"I think so, too."

"You might get your body back."

"Yes." Fier canted sideways, leaned his shoulder against Petra's. Sunlight and piano keys and arms steady around him. "I think so, too."

Fier stepped first, then Petra, and though Fier walked slowly, Petra matched his pace and kept so close beside him that Fier could feel his wrist, his elbow, his shoulder grazing his with every few steps.

You have been hopeful before, and you have been wrong. You will always be wrong.

No shadows flickered between the trees. No half-formed monster loomed out of the path in front of them. Beside him, Petra gave no sign of hearing anything.

No one wants what you want.

No one wants that with you.

He could hear them on all sides, rustling like the leaves overhead – a constant and unwelcome susurration. With each step, the whispers echoed louder.

You'll change your mind.

He'll change his mind.

You're wrong, you're wrong, you're wrong.

But this walk was nothing new. Fier had made this walk every day of his life. He had listened to these voices from the moment he opened his eyes until the moment he closed them. He had woken to *you're alone, you're alone, you're alone,* and he had heard it through meals, through lessons, through the moonlit hours before he could fall asleep at night.

And he was so tired of listening.

Sunlight and piano keys and arms steady around him. Fingers laced with his. Even if the whispers never stopped, even if he woke to *you're alone* each morning, here to the contrary was proof beside him. Here was hope beside him. Here was love, given freely, given without expectation or condition.

There was no way out but forward. So forward he went, steady and sure, with Petra at his shoulder, and he did not look back. The end of the forest lane grew nearer and nearer, the speck of light larger and larger, and the whispers blurred and rose into a shout, a wind, a roar. Fier grit his teeth and would not listen and did not look away from the end so nearly within reach.

The trees fell away, melted back into the formless walls and floor and ceiling, but the end of the tunnel burned so bright it nearly blinded, gave off no heat, not even as they came within arm's-reach of it. The voices vanished and left a ringing silence in their wake.

Fier squeezed Petra's hand – a silent request to pause – and Petra slowed to a stop and turned to him, a question in his eyes and in the tilt of his head.

"Petra." Against all odds, his voice was steady. "Thank you."

"For what?"

"For everything. Just... everything. And you *are* beautiful. I want to you to know that. Don't forget."

Though the light left Fier dazzled, he could still see Petra raise his free hand, then hesitate. Slowly, slowly, he touched the pad of his thumb to Fier's cheek, brushed as light as falling snow at tears since dried.

"You will wake up," he promised, and Fier blinked back new tears. "And I will be there when you do."

Silent, jaw set, Fier nodded, and when Petra squeezed his hand, Fier returned the pressure twofold. Hand-in-hand, they turned and closed their eyes against the searing light and stepped forward together.

Fier

THE SUN ON HIS CHEEK. Wooden boards against his shoulders. A pinch in his stomach that he remembered meant hunger.

He felt so *heavy*.

Fier sat up so fast, the room spun, but this was his *room*: the bed – the trunk – the wardrobe – the window open to sheets of morning sunlight. He tore off his gloves and touched the floor, but even then he *knew*, and as the wood grain grazed his fingertips, he let out a long breath, his first real breath in three years, and dug his fingernails into the cracks between the boards. He pulled up the corner of the rug, found it rough and dense.

He touched his face, his hair, his clothes – the short fuzz of velvet, the liquid silk brocade. He pushed back his sleeve just to see the fabric wrinkle and found three thin white lines across the back of his wrist.

"Petra!" His voice was hoarse. "Petra, it's broken! It's broken!"

When no answer came back, Fier twisted, searching, but saw Petra nowhere in the room. As he shifted, the empty glass jar bumped against his foot. The room was empty, but he could see a hand limp and half-curled in the corridor, its owner out of sight beyond the edge of the doorway.

Fier stood – and canted sideways on legs unused to weight. He staggered against the bed and pushed himself back up. Half-running, half-falling, he stumbled across the room and into the hallway, skidded to his knees at Petra's side, cupped Petra's face in his hands –

But Petra blinked, was waking already. He tried to cover Fier's hands with his own, but Fier's were already gone – had found Petra's collar and the rough fabric of his coat, pressed against his chest just long enough to be sure of his heartbeat, touched his cheek again and found it smooth, grabbed his sleeve and caught his nails on the stitches near the cuff.

Petra managed to sit up and catch one of Fier's hands between his own. Fier dropped his free hand to his lap and sat still, as still as he could, but Petra did not return the examination. He simply turned Fier's hand over, as carefully as if he'd caught a butterfly, and ran a thumb over the ridge of Fier's knuckles. He found the three white scars and followed them along the curve of Fier's wrist.

"More than enough," he promised again. "Not your neck. Not your waist--"

But Fier interrupted him with a cry that quite failed to be a word and threw his arms around Petra's neck and resolved to never never never let go.

Epilogue

ONCE UPON A TIME, Petra would have said, then, had anyone asked, *a child was born to earth and sun. The child, the gardener, grew, and love grew, and a witch saw him one stormy night and said, "This love will be needed, but not yet, not yet." She left him a shield, and she let him go.*

Crisp autumn sunlight turned the flowers on the windowsill honey-gold, and the oak door gleamed almost auburn as Petra knocked upon it.

And once upon a time again, because their two stories had not started side by side, *a child was born to stone and glass. The child, the prince, withered, and love withered, and a witch saw him one stormy night and said,*

"This love will be needed, but not here, not here." She left
him a shield, and she let him go.

And the rest, oh, the rest, we wrote together.

Though Petra had not been sure she would be
home this late in the morning, the scrape of a chair
from within marked the rise of the cottage's occupant
from her desk. Brisk, military footsteps proceeded the
likewise-brisk inward pull of the door.

"Petra?" Sir Eckhart seemed, naturally, puzzled
by his presence there, but already her gaze slid away
from him to the other of her two visitors, to the one
partially hidden behind Petra, and as recognition
dawned, and as Fier's hand tightened around his
own, Petra added what hardly needed to be said:

"He's home."

A RESOUNDING THANK YOU goes to my mother, my father, and my step-mother for their readership, support, and advice on absolutely all matters; to Karen Lucia for her editing and advising; and to Betsy Peterschmidt for her ebullient read-through of the final draft and for her support as both a lifelong friend and creator.